# Falling for the Fifties

# Falling for the Fifties

## The Back Inn Time Series

## Book Two

## Stephenia H. McGee

Cover Design: Roseanna White Designs
Images used under license from Shutterstock.com.

**Library Cataloging Data**
Names: McGee, Stephenia H. (Stephenia H. McGee) 1983 –
Title: Falling for the Fifties/ Stephenia H. McGee
232p. 5 in. × 8 in.
Description: By The Vine Press digital eBook edition | By The Vine Press Trade paperback edition | Mississippi: By The Vine Press, 2021
Summary: What would you do if you finally found Mr. Right…in the wrong time?
Identifiers: LCCN: 2020950394| ISBN-13: 978-1-63564-058-8 (trade) | 978-1-63564-055-7 (ebk.)
1. Christian Fiction 2. Time Travel Romance 3. Historical Romance 4. Clean and Wholesome Romance 5. Time Travel 6. Religious Fiction 7. Inspirational Romance

Dear reader,

As a historical fiction writer, I've always wondered what it would be like if I could travel back in time and get a firsthand glimpse of the eras I love to read about. Thus, the idea for this series was born. It's a fun way to imagine the impossible.

Please keep in mind, dear reader, that a *story* is all this is meant to be. It is not meant to spark a theological debate on whether God would allow the miracle of time travel. The Bible tells us "Man's days are determined; You [God] have decreed the number of his months and have set limits he cannot exceed" (Job 14:5) and "My times are in your hands" (Psalm 31:15).

Several of the things regarding the time travel in this story are not possible, but it allows us to suspend what we know to be true to simply enjoy the fictional freedom of the *what if…?* So, come with me, imaginative reader, and together let's go see what it might be like to "step back *inn* time and leave our troubles behind"!

Happy reading!
Stephenia

# One

 rue love no longer existed. If Maddie Palmer hadn't known that before tonight, she was certain now. She pushed a sweaty lock of milk chocolate hair from her face and tapped her foot on the brick sidewalk outside of what, earlier this morning, she'd hoped would be a nice restaurant. Instead, her self-proclaimed foodie date had invited her to a two-star dive at best. Heaving a sigh, she kept her back to the rundown exterior of The Crab Shack and watched the little blue dot that indicated the current location of her rideshare. Good thing she'd insisted on meeting Mr. Wrong at the restaurant. Too bad she'd let her friend Darla borrow her car.

She swiped off the app and pressed the green talk bubble for messages. She tapped Darla's name, and her thumbs pecked out a quick text.

*Get everything worked out?*

> *Yeah. All good. Just parked your car. Keys in the usual.*

*Thanks.*

*Shouldn't you be paying attention to your date?*

*Date over.*

*Bummer.*

They'd talk about the details later. She pulled up the rideshare app. What in the world was taking this guy so long? Her phone dinged again.

*So much for online dating?*

Maddie withheld a snort. If Darla only knew. A last-ditch resort, she hadn't really expected to find love online any more than she'd expected to find a platinum record bearing her name hanging on her wall. But really. Did no decent men exist anymore?

*Never again. From now on, I meet creeps BEFORE I agree to have dinner with them.*

*Ouch. Dish over brunch tomorrow?*

*Can't. Anniversary party for my grandparents. Supper Sunday?*

*You got it.*

Yep. No more online dating. Tonight's selection from the loser menu featured a handsy slimeball who suggested they ditch dessert and head back to his basement apartment instead. She checked her watch.

Seven twenty-three. Shortest date ever.

Maddie dropped her phone into her purse and shifted her weight in her heels. She'd even dressed up for the guy. Once she'd turned down his invite, he hadn't even offered to drive her home. Not that she would've accepted. But still. Being left standing on the curb stung.

She should have known better. So what if her roommates Kate and Darla had both found great guys online? They obviously had better luck with men than she did. Bad relationships just ran in her family.

Except for Nana and Pops, of course. But that was different. They had what that movie *The Princess Bride* called *true love*—the kind only one couple in a million found. Good for them, but it seemed the rest of her family lost out on the odds.

Chiding herself for the thought, Maddie said a quick prayer for forgiveness. Bitterness wasn't very becoming.

Her purse vibrated, and she dug her phone out. A picture of her grandmother's smile caused one of her own. Maddie slid her thumb over the screen and connected.

"Hey, Nana!" She forced more cheer into her voice than the moment warranted, but she didn't want her grandmother to worry on the eve of her big night.

"How'd your date go?"

Right to the quick. Maddie cringed. "Not as well as I'd hoped."

Nana sighed, her breath carrying pity through the phone line. "Another dud, huh?"

Maddie forced a laugh. "Guess all the good ones like Pops were scooped up a long time ago." Best change the subject before Nana started plotting which of her knitting club pals had a grandson no one had claimed. "Do you need me to bring anything for the party tomorrow?"

A blue economy Honda slowed, and Maddie leaned forward, looking for the logo of the car service. Before she could move, two people bounded out of the sagging restaurant hand-in-hand and slipped inside.

"No, Sadie has it all covered."

Of course she did. Aunt Sadie practically lived for party planning. "Well, if you think of anything, let me know."

Another economy car turned off the busy highway bearing the right logo, and Maddie stepped forward. After confirming her ride, she slipped into the back seat.

"Why don't you come down early?" Nana said. "You and I can spend a little time together before the party."

Warmth tingled through her. Even with her big sixty-fifth wedding anniversary, Nana had time for her. Nana always had time for her. Maddie didn't want to be a burden, but… "I'd love to. Thank you."

"Good. Let's have coffee at seven. See you then!"

Nana clicked off before Maddie could protest. Seven? Didn't Nana remember Maddie had a three-hour drive to get from her apartment in Madison, Mississippi, to Nana's quaint little house in Ocean Springs on the Gulf Coast? She checked her watch again. Seven forty-six.

If she packed quickly enough, she could be on the road by eight-thirty, nine at the latest. But that would put her at Nana's house at midnight. She did a quick Google search. Probably better find a hotel.

The third ad down caught her eye. Huh. She'd never seen that one before. Maddie clicked on the cheery Victorian and read, "The Depot."

"You need something, ma'am?" The driver, a clean-cut man in his fifties if she had to guess, glanced at her in the rearview mirror.

"No. Sorry."

Maddie glanced back down at her phone. *Step back "inn" time and leave your troubles behind.* Cute. She scrolled through the pictures of sweeping porches, a large library, and period-decorated rooms. Why was she even looking at a place like this? She needed to find a cheap motel.

The driver made a turn and hit the interstate. But this place was only about a half mile down the same stretch of picturesque beachfront road as Nana's house. That would make her morning easier.

She stopped gawking at the pictures and clicked on the link to the room rates. A pop-up block appeared, asking for her name and date to arrive. No required email. At least she wouldn't get spammed just for wanting to know the price of a room. She put in her name and today's date and pressed her finger on the "check availability" button.

The car came to a stop in front of her apartment building, and Maddie gave the driver the guest code to open the gate. She opened the rideshare app and gave the quiet man five stars for not bugging her with conversation or weird music. She stepped out and headed up the stairs, her heels clicking.

Inside, she dropped her purse on the kitchenette counter and pulled up the B&B again. No way. Anniversary Special!

*Join us for The Depot's anniversary weekend and get your room 75% off.*

Less than fifty bucks for the room? That was some special. Even she could afford that. Maddie placed the call and spoke to a pleasant woman who assured her she had one room available with Maddie's name on it. Even said she'd wait up to check her in. Talk about luck.

Twenty minutes later, Maddie hit the road.

*On September 26, 1955, Snowcloud Five, a U.S.*

*Navy P2V Neptune weather reconnaissance airplane flying out of Guantanamo, Cuba, was lost in Hurricane Janet, 300 miles southwest of Jamaica. The Snowcloud Five flew into the eyewall as Hurricane Janet continued to strengthen. Last transmission: Navy Reconnaissance Flight 5U93, observation number five, at 1330 GMT. Present weather light intermittent showers, past weather same, overcast and some scud below, surface pressure 1,003 millibars. Surface winds 050 degrees Northeast, 45 knots. Beginning penetration.*

Nathanial Hall leaned back in his chair and rubbed his temples. He checked the clock. Almost midnight. He had to report at 0700 tomorrow. He blinked and forced his eyes to focus. Before he could go to bed, he needed to finish this chapter on flights that had been lost to the storms.

A light knock sounded on his door. He marked his place, stretching as he crossed the plush carpeting to the door. He opened it to find Mrs. Easley, the lady who ran his temporary home at this B&B, smiling broadly at him.

"I have another guest arriving soon." She beamed at him as if the news was worth interrupting his studying.

"Um, that's great ma'am." He waited, but she said nothing else. "Did you need something?"

She shook her head. "Just wanted you to know she'd be coming in late. Room right next to yours."

The innkeeper was decidedly odd. But Keesler's temporary lodging had been filled due to all the training going on. Besides, her rates left a nice chunk of per diem in his wallet. "Thanks for the heads-up."

"You like music, right?"

What? "Yes, ma'am."

Her eyes twinkled. "I thought so. I'll see you when you get back."

With that odd pronouncement, she bounded down the hall with the ease of a much younger woman, her gray hair bouncing.

Weird. Nathanial closed the door and sat at the small antique desk again. Two months of training, and tomorrow he'd take his 7-level exam. Then it would be back to Sheppard Air Force Base in Texas. Unless of course he was selected to fill the vacancy in the 27th Weather Recon.

He could stick around for some quick house hunt-ing. Short-notice transfer orders would give him only thirty days. Not that he had much to move. He pictured a bungalow by the water. Nothing too big. Maybe—

He cut the thought short. He had to ace this exam first. Otherwise, all his planning meant nothing.

The Hurricane Hunters. His mother called his goal insane. He called it saving countless lives. Nathanial focused on his book again. History. Why did the last thing he needed to study have to be history? He rubbed his temples and tried to focus.

*Hurricane Flossy moved into the Gulf of Mexico as a tropical depression on September 21, 1956, and became a tropical storm on September 22 and a hurricane on September 23. Hurricane Flossy was the only hurricane to make landfall in the contiguous United States during the 1956 Atlantic Hurricane Season. Unknown in-flight complications cost the lives of the five-man crew on the B-29 "Magnolia Mayhem" of the 27th Weather Reconnaissance Squadron. The pilot, Major Robert MacBride, and his crew flew into the eyewall at—*

A door slammed, rattling his focus. What in the world? He shook his head. Must be the woman coming in late. No wonder Mrs. Easley had warned him. She entered like the hurricane he was supposed to be studying.

Something bumped on the other side of the thin wall. His senses heightened. Was she okay? Surely no sane—or sober—human being made that much noise getting settled into a room. He stepped closer to the wall, listening. He didn't want to be weird, listening in on someone, but if something was wrong…

Another bump, followed by a grunt. He turned to face the wall, and a shimmer of light caught his attention.

What in the Sam Hill—?

The mirror, the same one he'd checked his reflection in that morning, shimmered like rippling liquid metal.

"What in tarnation?" A feminine voice said through the flickering glass.

Nathanial blinked slowly. Then again.

He'd gone way too long without a good night's sleep.

Maddie dropped the heavy suitcase, which—thanks to the missing wheel—immediately toppled over and crashed against the wall. She grimaced. She'd probably woken up the entire inn. This place had to be packed with their anniversary weekend special.

Probably with a bunch of honeymooners. Or couples on a weekend getaway. Maddie rolled her eyes. No wonder the woman checking her in had watched her with such interest. She was probably the only single person to book a room on "anniversary weekend."

She could see why. Pretty place. The floral Victorian wallpaper wrapped the room in a calming light blue, and the heavy wooden furniture accomplished the touted motto of allowing a guest to feel like she'd stepped back in time. Leaving her troubles behind…? Well, that would take a lot more than a fluffy mattress and some antique furniture.

Wrangling her suitcase over to reach the zipper,

Maddie blew hair up her forehead. Gracious sakes. She was only staying the weekend. Her monstrous suitcase said otherwise. So much for being decisive. She'd thrown half her closet into the bag and figured she'd choose what to wear to the anniversary party later.

Carrying the load up the staircase had proved her crippled decision-making skills seriously needed attention.

Maddie rifled through the wad of clothes until she located a pair of cotton shorts and a loose tank top. Gathering her pajamas under her arm, she slipped off her sandals and headed toward the bathroom. The thick blue rug felt nice under her toes, and she stepped off the softness and onto cool, polished floors.

Movement caught her eye. What was that? Her pulse quickened, and Maddie clutched her pajamas tighter. Did something move in that mirror?

Ridiculous. She'd only seen herself. Still, it seemed odd. She took a step closer. The wavy glass of the old mirror hanging on the wall rippled.

No way.

She took a step back. She must be more tired than she'd thought. She blinked, and the glass cleared. Yep. Time for bed. She started to turn, but her reflection caught her attention again.

"What in tarnation?"

Maddie dropped her clothes and stepped closer, enthralled by the strange version of herself staring back at her. She lifted her hand, and the reflection did the same. It was her face, but rather than her hair pulled into a ponytail, the shiny locks had been twisted into two large swoops at her temples. Bright red lipstick parted as her jaw dropped.

She fingered her neck, feeling nothing. But the reflection toyed with a set of pearls settled at the base of her throat.

Maddie reached forward. So did her reflection.

She brushed her fingers along the silver frame. Immediately, white-hot heat seared up her arm. She stumbled. Lost her balance.

And everything went black.

# Two

What time was it? The thought brought Nathanial bolting upright. As he tried to get up, his feet tangled in the covers on the high Victorian bed. He lost his balance and tumbled out, landing face first on the rug. Groaning, he rolled to his side.

Why hadn't his alarm gone off?

Judging from the sunlight streaming through the lacy curtains, he'd be late for sure. And he couldn't be late. Mind scrambling, he threw open the closet and snatched his blues from the hangers. Of all the days to have to wear blues instead of his BDUs. Good thing he'd pressed everything last night. He buttoned his blue shirt in blind haste, barely even checking his gig line to make sure his belt was straight. He brushed his teeth, grabbed his hat and wallet, and jogged down the stairs. He cut a glance at the massive grandfather clock sitting in the foyer.

Six twenty-three.

"Mr. Hall!"

Mrs. Easley. He didn't have time for her this morning. He'd just have to pretend he didn't hear her and ask forgiveness later. He dashed out the door and down the front steps, not bothering to throw on his cap. He jarred to a halt.

Where was his Jeep?

"Mr. Hall!" Mrs. Easley called from the porch. "I can give you a ride."

He ground his teeth. "Where's my Jeep?"

Clicking footsteps hurried out behind him. "Best you get in the car, Mr. Hall, if you wish to be on time."

Barely glancing at the woman in a calf-length belted dress, he gave a curt nod and spun on his heel. Around the side of the grand Victorian, a shed with a manual-lift garage door held a wood-paneled station wagon straight out of the "Leave It to Beaver" era.

Not forgetting his manners even in his haste, he popped open the driver's door for her and then skirted a variety of gardening tools at the front of the behemoth to hop in on the other side. He was buckled before she slid onto the seat.

The engine roared to life, and the whale of a vehicle inched out of the garage. Nathanial looked at the woman across from him. He blinked, noticing her for the first time. Had her hair gotten darker? He could have sworn she'd had much more gray than the few streaks sticking out from under her round, flat hat. She looked a good ten years younger, if not more.

She smiled at him, her gloved hands resting calmly on the steering wheel as she turned onto the road. "This may be a difficult day for you, Mr. Hall. But remember, God works all things according to His plan."

He rubbed his forehead. Too bad God's plan seemed to involve him having been too tired last night to set his alarm clock. Come to think of it, he hadn't even seen the clock on his nightstand this morning.

Elvis Presley's distinctive voice crackled through the speakers. He inwardly groaned at her music choice but tried to force his foul mood aside. Not this woman's fault he'd overslept, and she had been kind enough to drive him. He offered a nod in response to her statement, which seemed to satisfy her.

Mrs. Easley was a kind, though decidedly odd, woman.

"Do you have security cameras on your property?"

"Too modern," she said, her eyes not leaving the road.

Of course they were. How could a person effectively step back in time with things like pesky modern necessities? How was he going to find out what happened to his Jeep? He turned his focus onto the glitter of the early morning sun on the Gulf of Mexico. It'd be nice to be stationed here, closer to home and family.

"You worry far too much. Everything will work out just fine."

Nathanial cut a sideways glance at her as she slowed for a stop sign. Work out fine? The cryptic tone to her voice grated on him. She hadn't seemed surprised by his missing vehicle. Almost as though she'd been expecting something. "Do you know what happened to my Jeep?"

"Not to worry. I'm sure your truck will turn up again soon." She flashed a smile.

This woman was as nutty as a can of Planters.

The muscles in his jaw tightened. He'd file a police report after his exam. He glanced out the window again. "Why aren't we going over the I-10 bridge?"

"Not to worry. I'll get you there on time."

He wanted to argue, but what choice did he have? He was at her mercy. The roads seemed strangely quiet this morning. A sleek black car rolled by. Was that a fifties-era Studebaker? He checked his wrist, but he'd forgotten his watch. He'd have to double-time it.

Whoa. Was that a Plymouth Belvedere? The red-and-white car was in pristine shape. Mrs. Easley turned off the beach boulevard and took a right at The White House Hotel. The parking lot was packed with classic cars. Must be some kind of car show going on this weekend.

They pulled up to the gatehouse, and Nathanial fished around in his pocket for his ID. He palmed the card as Mrs. Easley rolled down the window.

A male voice chuckled. "Got your mom to bring you in today, Captain?"

What? He looked up at the grinning face of a man dressed in olive drabs with an MP armband wrapped around his bicep. What in the world? Before Nathanial could say anything, the man waved them through the gate and looked at the car behind them. Nathanial glanced in the side mirror.

A pale blue Bel-Air? His skin tingled. Something was wrong. "Did you see that?"

"See what, dear?"

"The MP at the gate. He should be in BDUs. And all these cars—"

"Do I turn here?" She waved a gloved hand.

Right. He had to focus. She rolled past Meadows Drive. "Take a left up there at H Street."

She followed his directions, swinging the station wagon at a stop sign. Hadn't there been another building over there? Nathanial rubbed his eyes. Had he cracked under the pressure and lack of sleep?

He waved her to a stop. "No POVs past here. You'll have to drop me off and make the block." He pulled on the car handle.

"POV's?"

"Personally owned vehicles. Thanks for the ride." He slammed the door and jogged toward Hanger Road. He'd definitely owe her an apology. His mother would string him up by his ear if she knew how rude he'd been. But right now, he had to get to his test.

Late wasn't an option. He jogged past several airmen dressed in olive drab, their caps pulled over greased hair. The weird sensation in his stomach grew. Something was wrong.

Not knowing what else to do other than move forward, he burst through the doors at the training center and hurried down the hall to his classroom.

Sweating, he slowed his rapid pace. He opened the door and stepped inside.

Rows of young airmen—all dressed in olive drabs—sat at attention in their desks, facing the front. Nathanial halted. Had he gotten the wrong room? He could have sworn—

"Instructor." A blond man on the front row rose and saluted. "Class present and accounted for, sir."

Nathanial's mouth went dry. Instructor?

Maddie threw her arm over her face in an attempt to block out the pesky sunlight. What time was it? She was supposed to be at Nana's at seven. Then again, Nana knew her better than anyone and wouldn't really expect Maddie to show up before seven-thirty, eight, if her head kept pounding like this.

What had happened? She'd had a super weird dream about seeing herself dressed in a vintage costume in the mirror. Then there had been a painful burst of light. She didn't remember anything after that.

But hadn't she gone to the mirror *before* getting ready for bed? Or had that been part of the dream? No. She remembered coming into her room and digging through the suitcase.

She rubbed her eyes to clear them of lingering sleep. Obviously, she'd gone to bed at some point. She threw off the covers and sat up.

Uhhh…

This wasn't her room at the quaint little Victorian B&B. The small room held mid-century modern furniture crammed into the corners of powder-blue walls.

Pulse quaking, she jumped up. Where was she? Still dreaming? She rubbed her eyes again, but the room remained. Phone. Where was her phone?

She checked the squatty nightstand. No charger. No phone. Where was her suitcase? Panic rising, she placed a hand over her galloping heart. Think. She had to think. Maybe she'd just wandered into another room at the B&B.

Yeah. That had to be it. She'd just let herself into someone else's room. Without a key. And without remembering anything.

Pushing aside her panic, she pulled open the bedroom door. Instead of the Victorian hallway lined with gaslight sconces and paintings from various time periods, she gazed at the living room of a small apartment.

Blood thrummed in her ears. Had she been kidnapped? Would a murderer return at any moment? She took a quick survey of the room. Boxy couch in a sage green. Squatty coffee table. No TV. A radio that looked like something out of the 1920s. A writing desk with a typewriter sat against the wall. She stepped into the room and looked around, senses on edge. She moved over to the desk, looking for anything that might give her a clue where she was.

A funky cover of *LIFE Magazine* caught her eye. Weird. A woman in some kind of pointy black hat. She picked up the glossy pages.

*September 10, 1956. Siobhan McKenna in "St. Joan."* Looked to be in pretty pristine condition. Her kidnapper must be a collector. She filed the information away for her police report later. Sheer curtains covered the windows. She moved one aside. Below, a busy street bustled with several old-looking cars.

Must be one of those antique car shows happening. Good to know. That could help narrow down her location. Nerves skittering, she eased around the living room.

Two doors on the other side. Bedrooms? Was the kidnapper sleeping back there? A swinging door led to a tiny kitchen.

The little kitchenette held more vintage appliances, complete with a small curvy refrigerator. Her stomach lurched. She'd been kidnapped by a weirdo obsessed with the fifties. Would he put her in a ruffled apron and force her to fix him a pot roast? Her imagination jumped to a dozen creepy scenarios. She needed to escape.

ASAP.

Never mind that she wasn't wearing shoes and had on—she glanced down at herself—a long white nightgown. Better get out of here while she could. She darted back out into the living room and reached for what she hoped would be her exit.

She flung open the door and almost collided with a woman.

"Oh!" The woman stumbled back, then laughed. "I was just about to knock."

Maddie gaped at her. Was this the kidnapper? This well-dressed young woman who looked like she blended seamlessly into the vintage apartment?

Maddie took a step back. Could she take her? She wasn't a fighter, but desperate times and all…

"Am I early?" The woman frowned, dark brown eyebrows dipping toward her pert little nose.

Looking as confused as Maddie felt, this woman couldn't be a threat. And she seemed as if she'd planned to be here. Peachy complexion and warm brown eyes, she looked kind. And—huh.

Something about this woman looked eerily familiar. Had they met before?

The woman patted a pink pillbox hat on her curled hair. "Eight o'clock, right?" She beamed. "I'm Sue Ellen Cartwright. Responding to your request for a female roommate?" Her tone pitched up at the end as if Maddie might suddenly remember who she was.

Mouth dry, Maddie held open the door, the reason the woman looked so familiar immediately slamming into her.

Sue Ellen Cartwright was her grandmother's maiden name. And this woman looked exactly like the woman in the photograph of Nana and Pops the year they married.

*Exactly* like Nana.

"Sorry." Maddie reached up to pat her own hair only to find her tresses cinched in curlers and wrapped in a scarf. What in the world? "I'm a little…disoriented."

*Hey, God? Little help here?*

The Nana look-alike shifted, seeming concerned by Maddie's weirdness. Who could blame her? But Maddie had bigger problems than seeming strange to this woman who looked very much like a younger version of her grandmother. And who shared Nana's name.

Maddie glanced back at the furnishings. The place almost made it seem as if she'd gone back sixty-five years into the past.

*Step back "inn" time and leave your troubles behind.*

The B&B logo surfaced in her memory, and she

sucked in a breath. No way. That was one hundred percent crazy. Still. There was also no way she was dreaming all of this. Right?

"Come in, please. Do forgive my lack of manners. Haven't had my coffee yet."

Sue Ellen appeared to relax a little and stepped just inside the doorway.

Maddie laughed nervously, running her hands down her nightgown. "Um, do you know the date?"

Sue Ellen clutched a vintage purse in her gloved hands. Dressed in a pink polka-dot dress, she could've stepped off the set of *I Love Lucy*. Maddie and Nana's favorite show.

"September fourteenth."

And not October sixteenth, like it should be. She scrambled through her memories. "September fourteenth…1956?"

The pretty woman laughed. "Of course."

Uh-oh. Maddie shook her head and wandered back to the couch, dropping onto the cushion with a weighty plop. 1956. Had she traveled back in time to just before her grandmother and grandfather had gotten married?

Why?

Her prayer about finding a love like her grandparents' surfaced. Was God giving her some kind of vision of what her grandparents' romance had been like? She straightened. Far-fetched. Totally. But then, considering her current situation…maybe not.

She motioned for Nana—Sue Ellen—to sit down. "Forgive me. I've had a rough morning. I probably made you more nervous than a long-tail cat under a rocker."

Laughing, Sue Ellen seemed to relax and perched on the edge of the matching chair next to the couch. "My mother always used to say that."

She knew. The phrase had been passed down through quite a few generations. She studied the woman across from her. "So, where are you from, Sue Ellen?"

"Tennessee, originally. My parents moved to the coast last year, and I came down with them. I always wanted to see the ocean."

Test one, passed. That was the exact story Nana had told her several times. "Are you working?"

"Waitress at the officers' club." She flashed a pretty smile. "You?"

Test two, check. Maddie filed through all of Nana's old stories. She'd lived with a roommate near Keesler Air Force base in Biloxi when she'd first met Pops. Worked as a waitress at the club. They'd gotten married after only a few weeks of a magical, whirlwind romance. "I'm a music teacher." At least she was. In the future. "But I'm currently out of work." Code for didn't have a job in 1956. All of this craziness was making her head hurt worse. Maybe she'd actually developed a tumor and all of this was a super-vivid creation of her mind.

Maddie forced herself to focus. Sue Ellen might be

the key to the answers she needed. What had Nana said about her roommate? For the life of her she couldn't remember.

Whoa. What if all along Maddie was the roommate? No. Too weird. Maybe. How could this day *get* any weirder? Wouldn't that be how time travel worked? Creating a loop?

The maybe-Nana woman looked uncomfortable again.

"Sorry." She stuck out her hand. "I'm Maddie Palmer."

No flicker of recognition. The young Nana took Maddie's hand and gently shook it, a smile twinkling her eyes. Nana always got that look when she found something Maddie did amusing.

Her stomach twisted. This was uncanny. Super weird. Words. She needed to sound at least somewhat normal or Nana wouldn't want to be her roommate. Wait. What if that changed things? What if Nana went somewhere else? And then she didn't meet Pops?

Or what if—?

"I love how you've decorated." Nana—Sue Ellen—gave her a sweet smile.

"Thank you." Who had actually decorated here? For that matter, what happened to the real girl who was supposed to be in this apartment?

Maddie rose and gestured to another door on the opposite side of the living room. "Want to take a look around?"

Might as well play along until she figured out what she was going to do.

Sue Ellen rose gracefully and brushed the back of her long skirt. Maddie let out a relieved breath. That would be the first thing someone would do when looking for a roommate. Give a tour of the apartment.

Except this wasn't her apartment. Taking a gamble, she grabbed the first of two doors on the other side of the small living room.

Oops. "This is the linen closet. As you can see." Maddie closed the door and slowly opened the other. Oh good. Bedroom. "And this would be your room."

Young Nana walked past her and took a quick look around. Furnished similar to the room Maddie had woken up in, this one featured pinks rather than blues. And rose was Nana's favorite color.

"This is lovely." She watched Maddie for a moment, and then, seeming to come to a decision, gave a quick nod. "I like it. Would you be willing to wait for my share of the rent until the end of the week? I won't receive my paycheck until then."

Maddie forced her mouth to work around the dryness trying to mummify her words. "Sure. No problem."

She was going to be sharing an apartment with her grandmother. Only her grandmother was her own age. A sudden vision of Marty McFly holding a fading photograph flashed through her vision. What if she messed something up and caused herself to no longer exist?

Whoa.

She rubbed her temples. Whatever was going on here, she needed to figure something out soon. What happened to that mirror? Maybe touching the frame again would zap her back to the safety of the present where she was supposed to be having coffee with a much older Nana.

"If you don't have plans today, why don't you come by the club?" Nana smiled brightly. "We could get to know one another, and I'll introduce you to a few of the girls."

A chance to see what life had been like for Nana at twenty? An opportunity to see how her whirlwind romance with Pops unfolded?

What did she have to lose?

# Three

Talk about a weird day. Was this how Marty McFly felt in *Back to the Future* when he ran into his parents? He'd also dropped into the fifties, right? Maddie couldn't remember. Question was, why was *she* here? Would anything she did affect the future? Change the past?

*Sure could use a little help down here. I'm up for an adventure, but this is a little nuts.*

Dressed in low-heeled pumps and a June Cleaver dress she'd found in the closet, Maddie threw the prayer heavenward and followed her grandmother's directions for the short walk to the officers' club.

Elvis blared from nearly every radio of the lumbering cars rolling down the street. Nana had always loved Elvis. If she remembered correctly, the legend had once performed at the airman's club and then later started dating a girl named June, whom Nana had known in passing. She couldn't remember whatever came of that.

She passed men and women on the street, all

dressed in suits or fashionable attire. A few men wore olive drab uniforms and hats. Soldiers from the base. No, Airmen. She should know better. Hadn't Pops taught her that soldiers were Army and sailors were Navy? Or was that ground pounders and swabbies? Didn't matter at the moment.

The salty sea air ruffled the hair of a little boy sitting on a bench eating an ice cream cone. Fascinating. Life seemed the same and yet different. She passed a massive white hotel filled with shiny cars she'd seen a few times at the local fair, whenever they had one of those antique car shows. She had to admit, they had a lot more flair than the vehicles today.

For that matter, so did the people. No women pranced by in skintight workout clothes here. Each one of them seemed to have taken care to perfectly curl and style their hair before coming to sit outside under the swaying palm branches on the hotel's lawn.

How exactly had she ended up here? It must have something to do with that mirror. She'd touched her reflection and had woken up as someone else. Well, not really. She was still Maddie Palmer. But this Maddie lived in 1956 and had an apartment in Biloxi. If she was in Biloxi, that meant she wasn't far from Nana's modern house—which wouldn't have been built yet—and close to the mysterious B&B.

She should probably head back to that inn and march right up to her room. Maybe touching the mirror would send her back to her own time. But then, how cool would it be to get to see Nana and Pops's romance for herself? It couldn't hurt, right?

She could always go back to the present before the party.

The guard at the base let her through with nothing more than a smile and nod. Surprising. Two turns later, she arrived at a sturdy block building with rows of propped-open windows. One sleek green car with flaring fenders sat out front, the metallic paint glinting in the sunlight.

Maddie opened the door and stepped into a cavernous room with a gray tile floor. One side held pool tables with low-slung lights, the other a section of round tables crowded with metal chairs. The center of the massive space sprawled before a stage at the back. Looked like an auditorium turned hang-out space.

Place felt empty. Not surprising at two in the afternoon. People probably had jobs. She ran her hands down the front of her cotton dress and contemplated snooping around to find Nana. How did these people function without cell phones?

And hers was probably lighting up with calls and texts from Nana and her family wondering where she was. Not good. She had to get back before the party or it would ruin everything. They'd be worried sick. She couldn't miss the anniversary celebration.

Young Nana appeared from a door behind the

eating area wearing an apron over her flouncy dress. "There you are. I was wondering if you'd changed your mind."

She almost had, actually. But then, what if she went back and ended up exactly when she had left? Then she would miss this chance to see what Nana had been like at her age.

Probably totally irresponsible of her, but hey, she wasn't the one who had magical time portal mirrors in her house. She should have a talk with Mrs. Easley for sure. Just, not right now.

Besides, if she'd fallen and hit her head and this entire thing was a coma-induced dream, what did it matter if she lingered?

"Sorry. Took a little longer than I thought to walk here." Not to mention she'd lost track of time digging around in the apartment and trying on all of the clothes in the closet. Including the low-shouldered dress she'd seen herself wearing in the mirror at the inn. The gown fit like it had been made for her. All of the clothes fit her perfectly, actually, making this entire experience even more weird.

Nana twisted her mouth to one side the way she always did when she wanted to say something.

"What?"

Surprise lifted Nana's eyebrows. "You sing, right? You said you were a music teacher." She blinked. "Unless you meant you play piano or something. Do you play piano?"

"Both, actually." Maddie laughed. "My dad made me take piano lessons for years. Singing is my real love, though."

"Perfect!" Nana clapped her hands together. "I'll go tell Mrs. Howard. Sergeant Zollar will be pleased we found a replacement."

"Replacement? Replacement for what?"

She followed Nana through the open space of what had to be a dance floor and through a door near the stage.

"The band for tonight canceled. Something about a sick guitarist and a blown head gasket." Nana waved her hand as though that answered Maddie's question.

Nana had better not be saying what Maddie thought she was saying. "Hold on. You don't expect me to sing because your band isn't coming, do you?"

"And play the piano. Maybe we can round up a few other musicians. We'll figure it out."

Maddie came to a stop in the hallway. "No way."

"No way what?" Nana smiled at her. "Pretty thing like you, and the fellows won't even miss the band." Her forehead crinkled. "But you are good, right?"

Three local talent shows, a handful of teen pageants, and the fact that her students and friends said so, but it wasn't as if she'd ever tried out for *American Idol.* "Um, I guess."

This seemed to be news to Nana, because she

cocked her head and thought a moment. "You can sing for Mrs. Howard first."

"What?"

Nana smiled that smile Maddie had seen her entire life. The one that left no room for argument because you wanted to do exactly whatever Nana needed. "You're a singer. We don't have anyone for tonight's dance. What about all the servicemen who are looking forward to some downtime?"

Dance. The one where Nana and Pops met and fell immediately in love. If there was no music how would they dance? Her skin tingled. Not good. "Um, well…"

"Wonderful." Nana grinned. "I knew you'd understand."

Stunned, Maddie followed her young grandmother down the hall, once again asking herself, *what's the worst that could happen?*

Nathanial had taught an opening class on aerology to a bunch of airmen who'd never seen a weather radar. He'd managed to keep his composure and conduct the class in a somewhat professional manner. Good thing the military structured everything. If he hadn't had a detailed instruction manual with an exact lesson plan laid out on his desk, he might not have been able to keep up this charade.

He closed the lesson book, leaving it square on the desk for tomorrow's instructor.

Or himself, if he was still stuck in this situation.

Nathanial pushed the thought aside and somehow managed to keep his cool as the last of the students filed out.

As the door banged closed behind the final airman, he let out a long breath.

Why hadn't he left? He probably should have turned around and walked right out of this crazy dream. But the second lieutenant had known his name and his field of study. The men in this room had inexplicably expected him to teach this class on meteorology skills and aerology. His field of study. Somewhere in that moment, he had decided that one of two things had happened. Either he was having the most bizarre, vivid dream of his life, or he was dead and heaven was not at all like he'd expected.

The third possibility was way too crazy to consider. He ran his hands through his hair and drew a long breath. The cars. The music. The men's uniforms. He'd stepped through a wormhole and ended up at Keesler roughly sixty years before he was supposed to be passing his final exam.

His sense of duty hadn't allowed him to run out of the room or let on that he didn't belong. And then the arrival of a lieutenant colonel to welcome Captain

Nathanial Hall to his first instructor assignment had completely thrown him for a loop. Regardless of the ridiculous situation he'd found himself in, he wasn't about to walk out on orders.

But now that class had ended, he had better get back to that B&B. Whatever wormhole had sucked him into the past had to have been activated by the mirror he'd seen doing crazy things in his room. And the time warp had something to do with Mrs. Easley, who had to have known what was going on.

She'd been far too calm and collected. What with his missing Jeep, driving him onto the base, her cryptic words. What had she done to him?

Whatever voodoo she'd conjured up, he intended to find a reverse switch.

Mind made up, he walked out onto the street and through the base, his chest growing tighter with each eyeful of what he'd been too rushed to notice earlier. The buildings, the cars, the men. He bustled past a long building with propped-open windows he didn't remember from his time. The officers' club. Looked different than the one he'd visited on occasion during his training, but it sat in the same location.

A woman approached on the sidewalk, snagging his attention. Her eyes darted everywhere, and she seemed as out of place as he felt. He slowed his steps a fraction. Long dark hair fell in waves over one shoulder of her calf-length dress. Creamy pale features set off auburn hints in her shiny locks, and he caught himself staring. The woman didn't seem to notice, so he allowed himself to admire her until she passed him.

Once past the gate and off base, he paused. The B&B was a twenty-minute drive from Keesler. A quick scan of the area revealed what he needed. A sign for the base bus.

Not five minutes later, a rounded metal bus lumbered to a stop and the bifold doors opened.

Nathaniel stepped inside. "Fare?"

"In the tub." The ancient driver nodded a grizzled beard toward a bucket mounted on the dash.

This was the fifties. A buck should cover the ride. He fished the bill out of his wallet and dropped it in, wondering briefly if his currency looked any different in this time or dimension than dollars did in his own. He settled down on the cracked vinyl seat and hoped this bus took him in the general direction he needed to go.

Stupid he hadn't asked. But he didn't really want to call any more attention to himself than necessary. Three airmen entered a moment later, and then the bus bounced away from the base. Thankfully, it turned onto the seaside highway and made the turn to cross the bridge over Biloxi Bay.

They pulled to a stop just over the bridge, and a few men exited. Nathanial leaned forward to address the driver.

"How far does this line go?"

"Where you headed?"

"East Beach Drive." At least, he hoped that was the same name.

"Don't go that far. Last stop's at Pershing by the park. You'll have to hoof it from there."

He mumbled his thanks and sat back in his seat. At least he hadn't had to walk the entire ten miles.

Count your blessings, his grandmother would say.

A few stops later, Nathanial exited at the park and turned toward the B&B and the woman who had tossed him backward a few decades.

A fifteen-minute walk later and he turned onto East Beach Drive. The beachfront street held fewer houses than he remembered. His nerves prickled, making his skin feel itchy. Had he really thought through returning to his room at The Depot? What if he touched that mirror again and instead of sending him back to the right time—where he would have already missed his test and failed to report—he got sent somewhere else?

A risk he'd have to take. He couldn't stay here, that was for sure. He let out a breath of relief as the large Victorian came into view. He bounded up the porch steps and tried the handle of the ornate front door.

Locked.

Weird. In the weeks he'd been staying here, Mrs. Easley had always left the front door open during the day. The hairs on his arm rose. He knocked, then rang the doorbell for good measure.

Nothing.

He lowered his head to rub his temples and noticed an envelope under his shoe. He stepped off the welcome mat and caught sight of his name in flowing script.

A single sheet of paper inside held his name at the top.

*Mr. Hall,*

*By now I'm sure you've realized you aren't quite in Kansas anymore. But don't worry, you are exactly where you are supposed to be. If you're thinking you can ske-daddle right back to where you came from, then I hate to be the bearer of bad news. Returning to your room won't get you anywhere. And I won't be back to open the house until the twenty-sixth. Bad weather is coming, as I'm sure you know. I suggest you make good use of the time and learn the lessons this opportunity has granted you. I have a feeling you can make a real difference. How about you start with the dance tonight at the officers' club? I hear the singer is pretty nifty.*

He read the letter three times. No signature, but it had to be from Mrs. Easley. He rubbed the back of his neck. He didn't want to break into the house. He had no idea what day he'd dropped into. She could return tomorrow or weeks from now.

Going to a party right now seemed completely irresponsible. But so did hanging out on the porch for an undeterminable amount of time. At least on the base he could figure out what day—and what year—he'd landed in. Then maybe he could put together a plan of action and come back prepared.

Waiting wasn't his strong suit. Best keep moving forward and take opportunities as they came. He trudged down the steps, crossed the manicured lawn, and hit the sidewalk.

At the end of the street, he turned back toward the bus stop. Looked like a bus ride back to base. Maybe, if he had a class assigned to him, he had lodging on base as well.

Otherwise, he had no idea where he'd find a room carrying only a futuristic driver's license and a credit card that most assuredly wouldn't work. What would he do for living expenses?

The mess hall and base lodging were his only hope.

A car slowed next to him.

"Afternoon, Captain." A forties' model black Ford rolled to a stop. "Headed to base?"

Nathanial leaned down to get a look at the driver. Major. He saluted. "Yes, sir. Sure am."

"Hop in. I'll save you your beer money."

Glad for the ride, he slid onto the seat and pulled the door closed. "Appreciate it, sir."

The dark-haired man Nathanial placed in his late twenties grinned. "Going to the dance at the O club?"

Looked that way. "Yes, sir." He shifted his feet.

"You?"

"Thinking about it." He dipped his chin. "Major Robert MacBride, Twenty-seventh Weather Reconnaissance Squadron."

Weather recon? Maybe this was why he was here. That or Nathanial had spent too much time reading history before he went to bed. "Captain Nathanial Hall. You're a Hurricane Hunter, sir?"

"Best squad in the force." He barked a laugh, and Nathanial joined him.

Something niggled at the back of his mind. "Are you a pilot, sir?"

"Sure am."

Robert MacBride. The name slammed into him, and his mouth went dry. "Uh, you fly the Magnolia Mayhem?"

The major laughed. "You been studying up on the Twenty-seventh?"

This guy had no idea. "Yes, sir. I'm an aerologist."

Major MacBride signaled and made a turn. "So you must be that new instructor."

Apparently. At least in this alternate universe. "Yes, sir." He scratched his chin. "You, uh, know what day it is, sir?"

Major MacBride lifted his eyebrows. "Should I?"

That sounded stupid. "Sorry, sir. I mean the date on the calendar. Seems I've…lost track."

The salty sea air whipped through the open windows as they made the turn past The White House Hotel. "Been that kind of week, huh?" He chuckled. "It's September fourteenth, 1956."

Despite the laughter in the man's tone, Nathanial was thankful for the specifics. 1956. Pieces of the puzzle connected, forming threads in his mind.

The fourteenth. Mrs. Easley wouldn't be back for *twelve* days. Almost two weeks to stay here and risk being AWOL or bust into the house and get himself back to the present.

The cryptic letter rose to his mind. *Bad weather is coming, as I'm sure you know… I have a feeling you can make a real difference.*

He cast a sidelong glance at the whistling man driving. If today was the fourteenth, then he had one week to figure out how to save this man's life.

# Four

Maddie fidgeted in the back hallway of the officers' club, sweat prickling at the nape of her neck. Beyond the door, sounds of people laughing as they gathered for the dance sent her stomach twisting into nervous knots. Why had she ever agreed to do this? On the other hand, she'd never see these people again. So if she fell flat on her face, who would remember?

But what if she messed up and Nana and Pops didn't dance? What if she was so bad that the entire event shut down?

She took a deep breath. Stage fright got the best of her. The lights, the people staring. Sometimes it was all too much. Okay, so it was *always* too much. That was why she would never make a career of singing. She couldn't get rid of the tightness in her stomach. Her dry mouth. She'd nearly stopped trying and settled for teaching instead. Not that she didn't love the kids. She did. Maybe one of them wouldn't be constantly paralyzed by performance anxiety and would actually do something more than local pageants and a few small theatre productions.

"Don't be such a nervous Nellie," Nana said, looking as bright and shiny as a new penny as she swept through the door to Maddie's hideout. "You'll faint clean away."

Maddie gulped. Exactly what she'd been afraid of. "Well now, Nan—" She cleared her throat. "Sue Ellen. You'd be nervous too in front of all those people."

"Pish-posh. They're about as easy going as they come. Stick to the good songs everyone loves and you'll have no problems."

The blood drained from Maddie's face, and she put a clammy hand on the wall to steady herself.

Oh no.

Almost every song she knew had been recorded in the 2000s. Not the 1900s. She was going to be sick.

"Are you all right?"

Nope. Not even close. "I…I don't know any popular songs."

Nana shook her head. "You're being silly. How can you be a singer and not know any songs?"

"Not popular songs. I bet every song I know you've never heard of."

Nana patted her coiffed hair. "Then sing old ones."

That only made the situation worse. "Like what?"

"The Tennessee Waltz?" Maddie shook her head. "Mockingbird Hill?"

"Nope."

"So no Patti Page." Nana quirked her lips to one side in thought. "Doris Day?"

Mouth dry, Maddie shook her head again. She picked through her brain, trying to think of any artists from the era she knew a song by other than Elvis, who at this point had just started rising to stardom. She had no idea which of his songs were out and which he hadn't even written yet. Besides, she doubted she could pull his music off.

An idea struck. "Patsy Cline?"

Nana looked at her funny. Right. "Walkin' After Midnight" wouldn't have been popular for another year or two. But she could probably get by. Except, the band wouldn't know the songs.

"What about the band? What songs do they know?"

Nana made a sour face. "The band canceled, re-member?"

"You said you'd be able to find some musicians to play with me."

Sue Ellen gave her a sympathetic smile. "Looks like it's just you and the piano."

Ugh! So much for hoping they could provide the set. "Boogie Woogie Bugle Boy?"

Nana's eyes brightened. "Yes! What else?"

*Think.* What other songs had she performed in that community WWII play a couple of years ago? Oh! And the Wizard of Oz. "I know a little Judy Garland."

"Perfect." Nana peeked out the door at the gathering crowd. "Make a list. Quickly!"

"Wait!" Nana turned. "Do you have any sheet music?"

With an apologetic smile, Nana shook her head. "Sorry. Can't you play without it?"

She could, though she'd rather not. "A few songs."

"That's fine. Stop worrying so much." With a broad smile, Nana flounced away, leaving Maddie to figure out where to find paper and a pen and how in the world to come up with an entire set for a dance.

This was nuts. Nathanial ran his hands down his pants and watched as the O club filled with men ready for a night on the town. Women with their hair wound into tight curls and decked out in form-fitting dresses with flaring skirts sashayed among the men.

Would the woman he'd seen on the sidewalk be here tonight? She'd come into this building.

He shook the thought away and leaned against the wall. What did it matter? He wouldn't be staying long. The fewer people he tangled with in the past the better. What if he messed with the space-time continuum? Or was that something that only happened in movies? If he did nothing, he knew an entire crew of Hurricane

Hunters would die. How could he let that happen when he could stop it?

Or at least try to?

He pushed off the wall and walked through the crowd, one of only a few men still in uniform. Where was the latrine?

Spotting a door at the back of the restaurant area near the stage, he took a gamble he'd find the restrooms somewhere in that direction.

A shiny jukebox blared out oldies, the kind of music his grandparents had loved. The sounds brought a pang of nostalgia. How long had it been since he'd let himself really feel the music? His grandfather had taught him to play the best of Sinatra and the Rat Pack. The fun Elvis songs. He sure missed that man. Hadn't played a chord since losing him.

Nathanial pushed open the door and stepped into a quiet hall. No sign for the restrooms. Looked like he'd chosen a door to a hall lined with offices. He was turning to leave when a flash of movement caught his eye.

The woman he'd seen on the sidewalk bustled out of one of the doors looking flustered. She wore a fitted black dress that dipped low on her shoulders and skimmed the calves of toned legs. Her face twisted into a scowl, but somehow the expression brought a smile to his lips.

"How do they expect me to do this? With no warning, with no—" She jerked to a halt as her blue gaze slammed into him.

Striking woman. He offered a friendly hello. "I'm Captain Nathanial Hall."

Her mouth moved. No words came out. She pressed her thin lips together, assessing him. "Hi. I'm Maddie. Maddie Palmer."

"Nice to meet you, Maddie." Or was he supposed to call her Miss Palmer?

She didn't seem to mind the use of her first name. She tapped her pen on a pad of paper. "You here for the dance?"

"Yes. You?"

Maddie flung her arms wide. "The band didn't come!"

Wow. This woman launched into a conversation like a fighter jet off an aircraft carrier.

"They want me to sing, but I don't know any songs from this…" She trailed off, eyes uncertain. "I don't know many songs they will like. Especially not enough to play for the entire dance." She twisted long graceful fingers together. "Oh, I don't know why I agreed to this."

Interesting. "Maybe I can help." The words came out of his mouth before he could stop them. "I've played a few classics."

Uh-oh. He winced, but she didn't seem to notice his slipup.

She brightened. "Perfect." She tapped her pen on her pad like a reporter preparing to take his statement. "What are your favorite songs from this year? Or last year?" Her pert little nose scrunched. "Or really any year, I guess." She shook her head. "What songs do you like to play?"

*Danger Will Robinson.* Warning bells went off in his head. He'd have to be careful not to list anything from the wrong year. Like any year after this one. He shifted his feet. "I like Sinatra."

Those eyes sparked with excitement, doing strange things to his stomach. "Do you sing?"

"Everyone sings." At her confused look, he chuckled. "But I'm pretty sure people would rather hear my guitar than my voice."

Now she tapped the pen on her chin. So much for making her laugh. "Think it's okay for a woman to sing Ol' Blue Eyes?"

Something in his chest skipped, and he grinned. A fellow Sinatratic? "Sure. Why not?"

Maddie nodded. "Great." A strange look flickered across her face. "How about you tell me exactly which songs y'all would like?"

He rattled a few off the top of his head, hoping they weren't ones that came out after this point in time. She nodded along and jotted them down, so he must have been better at remembering release dates than he'd thought. Obviously she knew the ones he'd mentioned.

"Thanks, Nate." Her warm smile brightened her face, and he didn't even care she'd called him the nickname he'd always hated. The smile faltered. "Oh. Is it okay I called you Nate?" Had his expression given him away? "Should I call you Captain Hall?"

He chuckled. This woman could call him whatever she wanted. "I usually go by Nathanial, but you can call me Nate if you'd like."

That flashing smile returned. He couldn't tear his gaze away.

"Maddie? There you are." A young woman with dark hair opened the door behind him. "Are you ready?"

Maddie gripped the paper in her hand. "Well, I'm not sure I have enough songs and—"

"It's fine." The other woman gestured through the door. "No one cares if you play a few twice. And I'm sure we can throw in a few instrumentals. They can dance to some classics on the piano."

Looking what Nathanial could only classify as terrified, Maddie nodded and took a step forward. "Oh! This soldier—" She shook her head. "Airman." She scrunched her face and threw up her hands. "Captain."

When Nathanial chuckled, her cheeks turned pink. Had he embarrassed her?

She shot him a look. "This man plays the guitar. Can he join me?"

Wait. What?

The other woman raked a gaze over him. "Do you know the songs Maddie wants to play?"

"Yes. He does." Maddie turned bright, almost pleading eyes on him. "Would you mind?"

He glanced between the two ladies staring at him. "I didn't bring my guitar."

The woman at the door waved a hand. "We have several. Come along then. Time to get this party going."

He hadn't played in a couple of years. His fingers were probably so rusty he'd make a mess of this for her and a fool of himself. But the look Maddie shot him kept all his better judgments stuck in his mouth.

The woman disappeared through the doorway, and Maddie grabbed his arm. "Thank you. I was terrified to go out there on my own."

"Sure. No problem. Though I have to warn you, I might be a little rusty. Haven't played those songs in a long time." The words slipped out before he realized what he'd implied, but she didn't seem to notice.

Maddie scanned the list again. "Which of these do you know the best? If you can cover Sinatra on the guitar, I can probably still remember my Judy Garland on the piano." She flopped the paper in agitation before he could read any of the songs. "What I wouldn't give for some sheet music, though."

Nathanial agreed. She beamed at him again, and his stomach flipped. When was the last time a pretty woman had caused him to take a second look, let alone sent his pulse racing? Not since he'd joined the force and had thrown all his efforts into rising through the ranks.

Maddie grabbed his hand, sending nervous energy pulsing though him. They marched through the doors together.

Hanging out by the rear of the stage, they watched the crowd quiet and turn their attention to a sergeant who stepped onto the platform and grabbed a giant metal microphone. The tall man welcomed them all and thanked them for their service.

Maddie fidgeted next to him, a bundle of fluttering energy. She was making him nervous. She scanned the crowd, eyes darting across the faces of those listening to the sergeant.

"Looking for someone?"

She jerked her gaze back to him. "Just an old friend. But I don't see him." Her delicate brows dipped. "He's supposed to be here."

"Let's welcome Miss Maddie Palmer to the stage!"

She gripped his arm, and Nathanial found himself offering her a smile of encouragement he didn't feel. This could very well be a disaster.

Her eyes snagged on someone and her face lit into a grin. "He's here." The tension seemed to melt off of her.

Nathanial followed her gaze, and his pulse skittered. Major Robert MacBride, the man who'd given him a ride here.

And the pilot who would die in Hurricane Flossy in eight days.

# Five

The music took Maddie by the hand and led her through the anxiety pumping in her veins until all her knots unwound and only the sound of the piano under her fingers remained. She probably should have sung something for the opening number, but as jittery as she'd been, the only cure had been to take a few moments for her fingers to fly over the familiar keys.

The ivories yielded to the stroke of her touch, the music swelling to envelop the crowd in a haunting tune in minor keys. When the last note lingered, she drew a long breath.

The crowd clapped, and the tension in her shoulders dissipated. She could do this. She positioned the vintage microphone stand closer to her piano. Inspiration struck.

Of course! How could she have forgotten *Guys and Dolls*? They'd practiced that set for her music class.

She launched into "A Bushel and a Peck," and the crowd cheered. Nerves skittering, she followed that number with another show tune.

Judy Garland's "Get Happy" turned out to be a greater hit than the songs from *Guys and Dolls.* Her fingers flew through "Over the Rainbow," and then darted to "Singing in the Rain."

She hardly looked at the crowd, too pleased she'd remembered enough songs after all. Looked like she'd hadn't needed to drag that poor guy along…uh-oh. She'd forgotten all about him!

Her gaze darted to the handsome fellow sitting on a stool holding a guitar and smiling at her. She missed the next notes and stumbled over her words.

Better keep her eyes on the keys. She finished with a flourish and motioned for the Captain—Nate—to jump into this next song. He lifted his dark eyebrows as though to ask what exactly she wanted him to play, but if he knew all the Sinatra songs he'd catch on. Flushed with the excitement of the music, she launched into Sinatra and Ella Fitzgerald's "Can't We Be Friends?"

She'd sung both parts of the duet before. The crowd probably wouldn't mind. But before she could finish taking a breath between lines, Nate's rich voice picked up Sinatra's part in perfect pitch.

Stunned, she missed another few notes on the piano and had to scramble to catch up.

Couldn't sing, her foot!

The words poured out of him like silk down a buttered spoon, and her thoughts lost all sense of traction.

Goosebumps rose on her arms. Wow. Smooth, gorgeous, and everything a woman would expect in a man from the postwar era. When men were manly. Sophisticated in a chivalrous and—oh! Her line.

*"What a bust,"* she sang, *"this is how the story ends. He's going to turn me down and say, 'Can't we be friends?'"*

Her eyes lingered on him as she sang, imagining the pain in the songwriter's heart as she found the man of her dreams only to discover he didn't want commitment. A man like this one? Could be a total heartbreaker.

She shook off the feeling and concentrated on the music, letting it seep into her soul and pull her heart along for the ride.

They finished the song in lingering harmony, and the crowd of swirling dancers cheered.

Nearly breathless, Maddie took a bow and told the crowd they'd be taking a short break. She needed a few moments to catch her breath after a song like that.

She slipped through the door behind the stage, Nate on her heels. Laughing, she collapsed against the wall. "Can you believe that?" She fisted her hand on her hip and flashed a mischievous grin. "And you said you couldn't sing!"

His brown eyes sparkled, doing something strange to her stomach. "The crowd was too into you to notice I can barely carry a tune." He shrugged. "Somehow I just couldn't help myself."

This man was what Nana would call a *dreamboat*. Dark hair cut close on the sides, a little longer on the top. Strong jawline, clean shaven. Straight nose. Slightly bushy eyebrows. He was the kind of guy who looked good without trying.

Solid and manly. Probably not the type to go get a manicure. And, good gracious, he looked good in a uniform. Her heart tripped over itself. A date with this man couldn't possibly be as disastrous as the ones she'd been on lately.

But, even though he didn't look like it now, Captain Nate Hall was old enough to be her grandfather.

The thought threw a bucket of ice water on her heated emotions.

Focus.

Tonight wasn't about her and her terrible luck with men. She was here to make sure everything went well with Nana and Pops, not check out a man she'd never see again.

He stared at her, a look in his eyes she couldn't quite define as the side of his mouth tugged into a half-smile. Heat rushed through her again.

But then…looking couldn't hurt, right? She *could* flirt a little. Enjoy the company of a man cut from the same cloth as Pops. Tough on the outside, full of marshmallows—especially for his lady—in the middle. She stepped closer to him, realizing he was watching her study him, and a strange sense of boldness gifted by being out of time zipped through her veins.

"Can't wait to hear you sing some more Sinatra."

Those warm brown eyes, flecked with little bits of green, lit with a smile. The tilt of his lips made mush of her insides.

"Which song is your favorite?" His voice, deep but not quite a baritone, washed over her, drawing her even closer.

Favorite? "How about you pick one for me?"

*Bold, Maddie.*

But she didn't care. She meant every bit of the suggestiveness in her voice. Would he choose a love song?

Good gravy on a flat biscuit. What was wrong with her? She sucked in a breath and took a step back. She needed to check on Nana. Focus on the task at hand. Not let herself get swept up in the gaze of one astoundingly handsome man.

Must have been what happened to Nana. Pops had made a striking figure, according to those old photographs she'd seen.

She took another step back to put some distance between them. No matter the flutters in her middle, she had to remember the focus of this crazy night. Nana and Pops and their dance. The moment when they fell in love. She wanted to witness that magic for herself.

She'd asked Nana how she'd known Pops was the one, but Nana's cryptic reply that she'd "just known" had never given Maddie any real answers.

She straightened herself and tried to appear professional. "Five minutes, and then you take the lead on the next set?"

Before he could argue, she scuttled out the door. Wow. She needed some distance from that guy. He did weird things to her.

She found Nana standing in the corner of the large room, laughing with a tall man in uniform. Relief filled her. Good. All was going as planned.

That relief left in a rush, however, when she drew close enough to realize the man Nana turned sparkling eyes on was *not* Pops.

Not good. "Hey, Sue Ellen?"

Nana peered around the man and waved. "Maddie! Come meet Lieutenant Cline."

Maddie offered a polite smile and gave the man a quick nod. She grabbed Nana by the hand. "Mind if I talk to you a second before my break's over?"

"Of course!" Nana promised the man she'd be back soon, and the women walked to the dining area for Maddie to grab a Coke.

"Whew." Nana fanned her face. "It's antsville in here tonight!"

Maddie scanned the room, taking Nana's term to mean something like as busy as an anthill. "Yep." Where was Pops? Catching sight of him, she nudged Nana with her shoulder. "See that guy over there?"

"Which one?"

"Tall. Dark hair. Dreamy." Okay, a little weird to refer to her grandfather that way, but she wanted Nana to notice, right?

Nana pressed her fingers to her lips. "He's a looker, sure."

"Why don't you dance with him? I've got some slow songs coming up." Or, at least she'd make sure Nate played a few good ones. Who wouldn't want to fall in love dancing to Sinatra's "Close to You"? Nana didn't remember which song had been playing when they'd danced—she'd been too focused on Pops—but surely Nate's smooth voice could set the mood.

Nana's eyes widened. "What? Ask a man to dance?"

"Be a bit progressive. He'll like it." A fact she knew for certain, as Pops had often enough told the story about the beautiful woman who'd waltzed up to him and asked him for a spin around the dance floor. She'd stolen his heart that very moment.

But how in the world had the story ever come to pass with the way Nana was vehemently shaking her head?

"Why not?"

Nana laughed as if Maddie had said something funny and shooed her toward the stage. "How about you focus on that cool cat up there?"

Maddie's eyes immediately went to Nate, who had stepped up on the stage and was tuning a fifties-something electric Gibson. "But you'll ask Robert to dance, won't you?"

"You know him?"

"Sorta." Okay, so yeah, that was a lie. She'd known the man her entire life. But then, she didn't know him at this age, so that meant she didn't really know him as the man here and now. As the man he was currently. So maybe not a lie exactly?

Nana laughed. "Snag yourself a date with the musician and maybe I'll think about it."

What? No. Nana was supposed to dance with Pops *tonight*.

Was her being here screwing everything up?

Nate watched Maddie step back onto the stage, all her boldness from earlier replaced with nervous glances and fidgety fingers. Seemed like one second she'd been raking her arresting gaze over him like he was a prime dessert, and the next she'd gone from lioness to fleeing gazelle.

But those moments when she'd had flashing eyes and an impish grin? Man. No woman had ever sent his senses tail-spinning like that. She'd asked him to pick a song for her. His mind jumped to "The Way You Look Tonight," because never had those lyrics better fit a situation.

But he was pretty sure that song came out in the mid-sixties. Too far out of this decade. Another thought struck, and he toyed with the strings. An earlier recording. One with lyrics that suggested that, while writing this song, Frank might have been feeling something similar to what had overtaken Nathanial in the presence of Maddie Palmer.

And if he'd never see this woman again, why not serenade her a little? Granddad had always told Nathanial he needed to learn to live in the moment or he'd miss the best life had to offer. Maybe if he hung around the fifties a few days longer, he could experience life in the moments he had with Maddie.

She settled back at her piano and placed her hands in her lap, then gave him a nod. He adjusted the volume on the amp and shot her a wink. His fingers found the frets as if they hadn't spent years without the feel of the strings beneath them.

He closed his eyes and focused on the melody of "People Will Say We're in Love." The words came easy, slow and smooth. He sang of asking the girl not to be too wonderful. Not to be too perfect. Because people would start to talk.

He opened his eyes and focused on Maddie, smiling as he sang. He plucked the strings to the simple tune, filling the club with the sultry sounds of one of Sinatra's early ballads. Couples gathered and swayed to the music, their conversations forgotten underneath the power of

Sinatra's lyrics.

Her eyes widened with each line, the bright blue like the clearest skies on an early morning flight. She'd asked for a song, and he'd given her one. One that spoke of lingering looks and unexpected feelings that hit a man square in the gut.

The way her lips parted, he'd made the perfect choice.

Then suddenly, her gaze snatched away from his and scanned the dance floor. Maybe he'd been wrong. Frowning, she zeroed in on each couple caught in the current of the song. Her focus landed, and he followed her line of sight.

Major MacBride gazed down into the face of the dark-haired woman Maddie had been talking to in the hall before they'd taken the stage. He glanced back at Maddie. A crease formed between her brows, and she stared at them intently.

The last line lingered in the air, but Maddie's eyes never left the couple. So much for serenading her.

If he were to guess, this lady was already in love with someone else.

*Six*

inally! Pops held Nana in his arms. Smiled down at her. Relief oozed like hot caramel in Maddie's middle. Everything was happening like in Nana's stories. The dance. The moment. The music.

They started to part.

Wait. No.

The music had stopped. Couples were beginning to talk and separate. Maddie swung a glance to Nate.

He stared at her.

Oh no. She'd totally spaced. His song had ended and people would leave the dance floor. What if Nana and Pops hadn't had enough time? Without thinking, she pressed her fingers to the keys and let them fly over one of her favorite songs, not even caring that it was decades prior to the song's release. Celine Dion's "It's All Coming Back to Me" filled the air, the melody enticing people to remain on the dance floor. Linger in the romance of the moment.

Nana gave Pops a smile, and he pulled her closer.

She glanced at Nate, who still stared at her. He probably thought she was terribly rude. Here she'd asked him to play, and she was edging him out after only one song. But he couldn't leave dead air like that. Not at such an important moment. She flashed him a smile as her thanks for playing. And he could pick the next song. But right now, she had to make sure her grandparents stayed on the dance floor.

Pops twirled Nana, and they took a dip. Magical.

Concentrating, Maddie watched her fingers dance over the ivories. Had they always danced to this song? Maybe Nana didn't remember which song had played because she wouldn't have known a song sung by a woman who hadn't even been born yet.

They twirled across the floor, two people alone in the magic of new love. Couples twirled around them, everyone smiling as they drifted by.

Why had she even been worried? As long as she played the piano and didn't sing any lyrics, no one would notice a song or two that didn't belong. She could play anything. Oh, but that wouldn't be fair to her guitarist, who wouldn't know those songs.

Nate held his guitar across his lap, his dark eyes studying her. What must he be thinking? That she'd tried to upstage him? She flashed him a smile he didn't return.

Oh no. She'd have to make it up to him.

Nana looked up into Pops's face, a sweet smile on

her lips. Perfect. Maddie played the chorus again to draw the song out longer, enjoying witnessing the magical moment they fell in love.

Something was off about Maddie Palmer. The woman looked as nervous as a feral cat. Her eyes kept darting to the dancers on the floor, her pretty face drawn tight in concern. The dance floor filled with swaying couples, though best he could tell, one couple in particular held her attention.

She flowed seamlessly from one melody to another, not even pausing before starting the next song. Wait. This tune was familiar. He strained his memory but couldn't place the lyrics. He leaned back in his chair, watching her. Maddie shot glances to the dance floor every few notes.

There must be a history with her and the major. A bad break-up, maybe? He'd seen women fly off the handle if a friend dated an ex. What was the story there?

It didn't matter. Maddie's business was her own, and he didn't need to be meddling with these people any more than necessary. He watched Major MacBride cross the dance floor.

Would saving his life and the lives of his crew alter history? Would Nathanial unravel some kind of space-time continuum by prolonging the lives of people meant to die?

Maybe. But he had to think that if God hadn't intended for him to save this man, He wouldn't have put him there. Why else would he run into the very pilot he'd been reading about? There had to be a mission in this trip, and saving the crew of the Magnolia Mayhem had to be his purpose.

Getting dropped into the past out of random coincidence wasn't an option he cared to consider. Because without a purpose, he had no mission to fulfill. And if he didn't complete what he'd been sent to do, then he might never get back home.

Nathanial preferred to believe in purpose. He sent up a prayer for wisdom, hoping the Almighty would let him in on a few more details of this unconventional outing.

The music finally drifted to a lingering note, and breathless couples parted. Maddie beamed at him, all of her earlier concerns strangely wiped from her face.

"What would you like to play?"

He nearly told her she could play whatever she wanted. She obviously didn't need him. But there was a look of hopefulness in her eyes that stalled him.

"Do you know 'Learnin' the Blues'?"

Of course he did. One of his favorites from Ol' Blue Eyes. He sighed. What could it hurt to play a few songs with a pretty girl he'd never see again? Rather than answer her, he grazed his fingers over the strings and then plucked out the opening notes.

The crowd let up a cheer. Apparently, he'd found a favorite. To his surprise, Maddie joined in on the melody, her fingers expertly melding her tune with his. She gave him an encouraging smile, and for a few moments, he forgot he couldn't really sing.

The crowd joined in on the chorus. Some still danced, others stood by the stage watching him. He lost himself in the moment. What did it matter if he embarrassed himself? He didn't have to work with these people. Didn't matter if he had the lasting respect of crew members. Not here. Here, he could let go a little.

They sang four more Sinatra favorites, and then Maddie picked up a couple of show tunes. He actually knew "Gentleman Prefer Blondes," and "Get Me to the Church on Time," which seemed to surprise Maddie. The woman did like her show tunes.

Finally, their musical night drew to a close. He rose and stretched his hands. His fingertips were sore, having lost some of the calluses that had once guarded him from the strings. But he'd enjoyed playing again.

Maddie rounded the upright piano and stood by his side. Grinning, she took a deep bow like the star of a Broadway hit. He withheld his laugh and joined her. The crowd clapped, and she gave them a little wave, then bounded down the stairs.

Nathanial propped the guitar on the chair and gave

the instrument a sentimental pat, then hopped off the stage.

"Hall!"

He turned to find Major MacBride striding toward him. "Yes, sir?"

"Need a ride? I'm heading out."

He cast a glance at the woman who'd so captivated him. Should he hang around and tell Maddie good-bye? Grab one more moment to see her smile?

Ridiculous. He would always have the memory of a beautiful singer and a night in the golden age.

Besides, if he didn't go with the major, he'd end up walking around base looking for lodging. He gave a nod and headed in MacBride's direction.

Casting one last glance back at the stage, he shook his head. He couldn't quite put his finger on the feeling that nudged the back of his mind, but he was fairly certain of one thing.

There was something different about Maddie Palmer.

# Seven

*L*ast night had been incredible. Maddie couldn't wait for Nana to arrive today and move into the apartment. Then they could dish about the dance.

She'd missed the moment Nana asked Pops to dance, but she'd seen the way they'd looked at each other. They'd fallen into each other's eyes as the music washed over them.

Totally romantic and everything she'd thought the moment would be. Just like a fairy tale. Maddie sighed wistfully and made a twirl in her long skirt. And she'd been there to see the magic happen.

A shadow darkened the sunny thoughts surrounding the events. Nate had disappeared as soon as they'd finished the set. She'd looked everywhere for him after they'd taken their bows, but he'd slipped off while she'd made a quick trip to the restroom. Why would he do that? Had he not enjoyed the evening as much as she had? Had he not felt a connection?

Would she ever see him again?

She breathed a long sigh. Did it really matter? He was from a different era. Why torture herself?

A knock sounded on the door and Maddie rushed to open it. "Nan—um. Sue Ellen! Come in."

Nana laughed. "I must look an awful lot like your friend Nan. That's the second time you've called me by her name."

Maddie merely nodded, letting Nana's guess stand. She'd better start thinking of her grandmother as Sue Ellen. Once or twice was forgivable. Too many times would be flat out rude.

Calling her Nan would be bad enough. Calling her Nana would seem like a whole new level of weird.

Sue Ellen carried two suitcases in her gloved hands and bustled past Maddie and into the living room.

"Is that all you brought?" Maddie eyed the two suitcases. The apartment was furnished, but she'd still expected Nana—Sue Ellen—to have more belongings.

"There's two more in the lobby. A nice fellow should be up with them shortly."

She'd left her belongings with a stranger? No sooner had the thought occurred than a male voice bounced through the open doorway.

"This the right room?"

Maddie waved the large man carrying two hefty suitcases through the door. He plopped them down and swiped a sleeve over his glistening brow.

"Whew. Young lady, you must have bricks in

those."

Sue Ellen beamed at the older gentleman. "And you were right kind to lug them all the way up here for me. What would I have done without my rock collection?"

The man tilted his head back and barked out a laugh. "You girls have a good day."

"You too, Mr. Harmon. Thank you again."

Maddie closed the door behind him. "Do you know that man?"

"Met him in the lobby."

Different times for sure. Maddie wouldn't have struck up a conversation with a stranger in the lobby, and she doubted any modern man would have volunteered to carry two heavy suitcases for her. Not that she would she trust him to come into her room if he had.

But then, men did hold doors for her sometimes. Mississippi still held on to a few lingering wisps of the forgotten age of chivalry. Southern mommas persevered by insistently instilling some of those traits in their boys. Manners stuck to some better than others.

"So." Maddie clapped her hands together. "Tell me about last night."

Sue Ellen grabbed one of the suitcases and strode to her new room. "What about it?" She laughed. "You were there, remember?"

"What about your dance with Major MacBride?"

Sue Ellen reappeared in the doorway. "You saw

that, huh?"

"Sure did. Looks like you asked him to dance after all."

Pink tinged Sue Ellen's cheeks. "The song started, and the friends he'd been talking to all coupled up and moved away. Poor man looked so out of place standing on the dance floor all alone."

Maddie grinned. "What happened?"

"What do you mean? We danced. He seems nice enough." Her eyes sparkled with humor. "I also danced with Lieutenant Cline. That man's feet can move like nothing I've ever seen."

What? No. Nana was supposed to dance with Pops and then—boom. Happily ever after. Why was she talking about some other guy? "Who?"

"Remember? You met him. We were talking when you took a break." Sue Ellen patted her perfectly curled hair, looking as pleased as a fifties woman in an advertisement for a new dishwasher.

Not good. Maddie shook her head. "Did Robert ask you out?"

Sue Ellen's eyebrows lifted. "How'd you know?"

Relief swept over her. "Good. When's your date?"

"I didn't agree to a date."

"What! Why?"

They stared at one another, Maddie's nerves on fire and Sue Ellen looking somewhat concerned by Maddie's outburst. She schooled her features into a semblance of calm. "I mean, you two looked over the moon for one another. Why wouldn't you go out with him?"

"Over the moon?" Sue Ellen gave her a dubious look. "I only just met the man. Good golly, you're a hopeless romantic."

The words felt like they'd slapped her. Every story she'd ever heard was that Nana asked Pops to dance. They'd fallen in love at first sight. Had she meddled and ruined everything? Maybe Nana was supposed to keep talking to this Cline fellow long enough to realize he was a no-good jerk, and Maddie had stopped that from happening.

Now Nana seemed like she was more interested in that guy than Pops. Not good. Not good *at all*. What was she going to do?

"You seemed to be making moon eyes yourself up on that stage." Sue Ellen propped her hands on her hips. "You sure you're not projecting your own swooning onto everyone else?"

Maddie grabbed one of the suitcases and tugged. What did she have in here? Mr. Harmon hadn't been kidding when he'd said the thing felt filled with bricks. "I'm not swooning over anyone." *You're the one who was supposed to be doing that.*

"Why not go out with him?" Nana asked.

"He didn't ask." And she had no idea where to find him, anyway.

"He's friends with Major MacBride. They left together."

Maddie dropped the suitcase on her toe and yelped. "Really?"

Sue Ellen laughed. "I'll tell you what. I'll go out with Major MacBride as long as you and Captain Hall tag along." A mischievous light gleamed in her eyes. "We'll make it a group thing."

Fix her mess and get to see Mr. Dreamy again? "For you, I suppose I could."

Sue Ellen laughed and pulled her into a quick hug. "You're the funniest girl I ever met. We're going to have a blast."

A headache pounded between Nathanial's temples. He'd half expected to wake up this morning back in his room at The Depot. The crazy day he'd had yesterday should have been a dream. But he was still in a small room inexplicably assigned to him at on-base lodging and not at the B&B.

He hadn't known where else to tell Major MacBride to drop him off, so he'd suggested the lodging facilities. He'd been floored when he'd asked for a room assignment only to discover one had already been given to him. The man on duty asked if he'd lost his key and then gave Nathanial a new one.

How did he have a class to teach and a room assigned to him in an era he didn't belong in? Only one explanation. He'd fallen, been shot, or lived through something else equally traumatic and was currently hooked to a bunch of tubes in a hospital somewhere. This long, vivid dream must be from a coma or some serious pain killers. How else would an entire life be set up for him here?

He couldn't make heads or tails out of any of it, least of all the emotions lodging in his chest. Maddie Palmer had throttled his senses. Her voice, her expressive blue eyes, the way she'd lost herself in the feel of the music. He'd been mesmerized, letting himself forget everything but the way she looked sitting at that piano.

He could only blame the crazy circumstances for making him act so completely out of character.

He placed his feet on the cold tile floor. A Saturday with nothing to do. For the last several months, he'd spent every available moment studying, punctured with a few breaks to hit the gym and burn energy. He'd thrown every ounce of his efforts into filling an assignment in the Hurricane Hunters.

What would he do with a free day?

He strode to the small closet, only half surprised to find clothing—presumably in his size. Two pairs of olive drabs and a set of blues slightly different than his own hung on wooden hangers. If this hadn't been a dream, surely someone would have reported him for being out of uniform with a different belt and set of ribbons.

Seemed no one had noticed. Another indicator he'd made all of this up. But if he had that kind of power, why hadn't he gotten himself the girl last night?

Probably because, even in his own head, he managed to make a fool of himself with women. Besides the uniforms, he found three pairs of slacks and three button-down shirts in blue, red, and gray. One three-piece suit. Two classy hats—one straw, one felt.

No jeans and T-shirts, and no athletic shorts. Guess he'd either have to find the BX or skip the gym. He pulled open a few drawers and found pairs of boxers and folded white T-shirts.

Hadn't he always seen guys from the fifties in cuffed jeans and tight white shirts with leather jackets and greased hair?

Looked like he'd be playing a role more like Sinatra in *From Here to Eternity* and less like Travolta in *Grease*. Fine by him. He pulled on the pleated gray trousers, paired them with the blue short-sleeved shirt, and finished with a black belt and a pair of shiny dress shoes.

He found a comb and made quick work of his hair, ignoring the can of pomade that sat on the dresser. A few moments later he headed downstairs and out into the morning sunshine. He paused to read the headlines of the Biloxi Daily Herald.

*Crazed Killer Captured with Burst of Gunfire.*

Nathanial shook his head and kept walking. Looked like some things never changed. He rounded the corner and found a bench. Probably a good idea to do a little recon and get the feel for his current situation. Besides, he couldn't think in that tiny room.

A man needed fresh air to settle his thoughts.

Massive cars cruised down the street, and children scurried around well-dressed women headed down the sidewalks on various errands. Men in uniform walked with purpose to one duty or another. After only a few moments on the bench, he grew restless.

What was Maddie doing today? He tried to picture the daily life of a fifties woman but came up short. Most of his experience with the era had been limited to watching *I Love Lucy* and *The Andy Griffith Show* during the summers with his grandparents. And he was pretty certain the real world hadn't been like the television shows. Not according to his granddad's old stories. He grinned to himself. Those stories had gotten considerably more interesting as Nathanial had hit his teen years.

Being like his grandfather was what had sent him into the military in the first place. Granddad had been a crew chief, working on the massive B-29 super fortresses and the B-52 bombers. He'd served in occupied Japan, the Philippines, and Vietnam.

After Nathanial had lost his father at age thirteen, Granddad had been his sole male role model. A tough man with an iron work ethic, a solid faith, and an abundance of wisdom. Nathanial could think of no better way to honor the man than to emulate him.

Granddad had been so proud when Nathanial had joined the Air Force. If only he could see him now. A thought suddenly struck. Could he? If he was in 1956, then Granddad was still alive. The thought lurched him to his feet. He could find him.

"Captain Hall? That you?"

Nathanial turned at the sound of the familiar voice. "Major MacBride. How are you, sir?"

Dressed in attire similar to Nathanial's own, the other man put his hands in his pockets. "Right as rain. What are you up to today?"

"Nothing much, sir."

The man eyed him for a moment. "I'm headed down to the beach. Want to come?"

Did he mean swim trunks and sunbathing? Nathanial didn't have anything suitable in his closet. But then, MacBride didn't looked dressed for the occasion either. "What did you have in mind, sir?"

He laughed. "The usual. Have a few drinks. Watch the girls hit the ocean."

Girls. "What about Miss Palmer?"

"Who?"

Nathanial frowned. Hadn't she said the two were

old friends? "Maddie Palmer? The singer?"

MacBride removed his cap and swiped his forehead. "Right. What about her?"

"You two aren't together?"

"What gave you that idea?"

Maddie. The way she had zeroed in on him and her friend dancing. He shook his head. "Never mind. What about that girl you danced with last night?"

"Which one?"

This was going nowhere. He laughed, but the image of Maddie watching them dance wouldn't leave him. He'd seen longing on her face. Caught the way her eyes shimmered. MacBride might not know Maddie Palmer, but she sure knew him. "What time do we leave, sir?"

"Just Mac is fine when we're not in uniform."

Nathanial smiled. "Yes, sir. Thanks."

He checked his watch. "Let's make it noon. We'll grab lunch at Hugo's."

Nathanial grinned. He'd been there as a kid, before it closed back in 2003. He'd love to see the pizza shop in its heyday. "Heard good things about that place, sir."

Plans made, the major sauntered off and left Nathanial to resume his brooding. Lunch at the restaurant famous for putting French dressing on pizza. Then an afternoon bumming around the beach. MacBride had mentioned women. Would Maddie be there?

Didn't seem likely. He pushed the image of her from his mind. He didn't need to be distracted by a pretty face. They didn't have a chance of a real future, and he had more important things to consider.

Like how could he track down Granddad in a time before the internet?

# Eight

The fifties diner didn't look anything like they did in the movies. Maddie tried not to be disappointed that she didn't see any girls in poodle skirts sharing a milkshake with greasy-haired boys in leather jackets.

A New York style pizzeria, the space held simple wooden tables with red chairs. A long bar ran along one side of the room surrounded by tall seats and filled with patrons waiting on their lunches.

The smells of cheese, tomatoes, and Italian spices hung on the air, tantalizing Maddie's senses. She did love a good slice every now and then.

Sue Ellen led them to a booth by the window. "You have to get the liquid cheese," she said without looking up from the menu. "It's all the rage."

Liquid? Maddie shrugged. Most any cheese was fine with her. She'd even eat mushrooms on the thing. Right now, she had bigger problems than pizza. Like how was she going to fix the mess she'd made of her grandparents' romance? And if she didn't, would it mean her mother would never exist? And if her mother didn't exist, then Maddie might fade out of the picture like Marty McFly.

She should have minded her own business and gone right back to her own time.

"Anything catch your fancy?"

Maddie didn't glance at the menu. "The women in my family like ours with pepperoni and pineapple."

Sue Ellen grinned. "Really? I thought I was the only one who ate pineapple on pizza." She scanned the menu again. "But I don't see any listed here. Keep it simple with pepperoni and cheese sauce?"

"Sure."

Smells of gooey cheese and New York style crust permeated the crowded space, and the sounds of several conversations created a pleasant hum around them. Was this place still open back home? Maybe she and Nana could jaunt over to Biloxi and visit. Would Nana remember coming here sixty-five years ago with her roommate? One who looked an awful lot like her granddaughter? How much would she remember of their time together?

Huh. Apparently, somewhere along the way, Maddie had given up on the dream theory and dived head-first into believing in time travel. She'd never taken herself to be someone to buy into the unexplained so easily. Maybe those UFOs in the tabloids weren't secret military planes after all. Maybe little green aliens really were watching them. Who could tell anymore?

She studied the woman across from her. Nana's love of pineapple pizza hadn't been caused by Maddie at a Biloxi restaurant. So Nana already liked the combination, which she would pass to her daughter and then granddaughter.

How much did Maddie have influence over? How many things would she change by being here?

*Lord, a little wisdom?*

She drew a long breath to calm her spiraling thoughts. Control was an illusion. She couldn't have prevented losing her father. She hadn't been able to stop her mother from leaving. She certainly hadn't sent *herself* back to the past.

When had she ever been in control of anything? No sense worrying over that now.

God had a plan in all of this somewhere. She'd just have to figure it out. Or not. Maybe she should simply relax and see what happened. If she wasn't in control anyway, why fight this current?

A cute waitress with blond hair in a ponytail bounded up and took their orders for two Cokes and a medium pepperoni to share.

"Well, look who it is." Sue Ellen leaned forward as the waitress turned away. "Your fellow from last night is here."

As discreetly as she could, Maddie turned to look at the door. Her pulse did a jitterbug, though she couldn't say why. Maybe the way Nathanial looked in slacks with his hat tugged low on his brow. Or the way he freed his locks from underneath as he glanced around for a peg to hang it on. Men in this time were so much classier than the guys back home with their video game T-shirts and holey jeans.

Sue Ellen laughed. "You're totally smitten."

Maddie whirled around. "I am not." Was she? No. That was silly. She couldn't be attracted to a man in 1956. Talk about crazy. He'd be at least Pops's age—if he was even alive—when she got back home.

But what if she never went home?

The idea dropped on her like a five-ton hammer. She had friends, a job she liked, and a family. She'd miss the first two. But if she stayed here, her time with Nana would be far longer than she'd have back home.

True, the woman would never know Maddie as her granddaughter, but they could be lifelong friends. Wouldn't that be even better?

But then what would she do when her mother was born, then…herself? Would she watch her life over again and end up being caught in a continuous loop?

Goodness, her brain would turn to mush if she kept up these questions. Like trying to stuff a ten-pound turkey into a pie tin, this time situation was more than her head could hold.

The waitress returned and set their bottles of Coca-Cola on the table. Maddie stared at the condensation beading on the vintage green glass. How did she figure out the right things to do or not do when every decision she made could turn the world upside down? Or, what if it didn't even matter what she did because destiny had already been written?

The questions pounded in her head, making her lungs constrict.

"Maddie? Are you all right? You've gone as pale as a sheet." Sue Ellen reached across the table and grabbed Maddie's hand. "I was only joshing you."

What? Maddie blinked, trying to clear the jumbled thoughts. She'd deal with impossible decisions later. For now, she needed to focus on Nana. "Sorry. Got lost in thought."

"About the captain?" Sue Ellen wiggled her eyebrows, and Maddie couldn't help but laugh. She released Maddie's hand, and her eyes drifted to something over Maddie's shoulder.

Maddie twisted in her seat and sucked in a surprised breath. Pops! She whirled back around. "Looks like he came with Major MacBride." A coy smile tilted the side of her lips. "How convenient."

Sue Ellen shook her head as though she didn't care that Pops had entered the room. Well, they'd just see about that.

Emboldened with the "live like there's no tomorrow" sense one got from being out of time, Maddie raised her hand and called to Nate. "Hey, fellows!"

"Maddie! What's gotten into you?" Nana gasped.

Maddie ignored Sue Ellen's flustered comment and continued to wave the men over. If she was going to be here, she might as well take advantage of the opportunities presented. She was more inclined to believe in providence than coincidence. And Pops walking into the same restaurant where they were clearly fell into the "providence" category.

*Cool. Thanks, God.*

Sue Ellen mumbled something about how a lady shouldn't be the one pursuing a man, but Maddie didn't have time to focus on the weird comment. Hadn't Nana always been the progressive type?

The men approached the table, and Pops dipped his chin in greeting. "Ladies. Nice to see you again."

Maddie watched Nana for any signs of swooning but saw none. She merely smiled politely and returned the dry greeting. Maddie darted a look at Nate, but he wouldn't meet her gaze.

Pops said something about seeing them later, but before he could move away Maddie blurted, "Why don't y'all join us?"

Sue Ellen gaped. Pops grinned. Nate's eyebrows dipped, and his mouth tightened. After a second, however, Pops took command.

"We'd love to join two lovely young women for lunch. Thank you for the invitation." He flashed Maddie a charming smile, and she couldn't help but laugh. Pops had always been likeable. The man could make friends with a stop sign.

The women scooted over to make room in the booth. Thankfully, Pops eased in next to Nana, who offered a shy smile as she moved her Coke bottle.

Nate settled down next to Maddie, and she caught a whiff of something. Something quite different from the scents of tomato sauce and yeast. Warm and inviting. Like pine and rain. She caught herself leaning closer to Nate and suddenly straightened. What was *that* about?

Nate tapped his finger on the table, clearly uncomfortable. What had happened to the carefree man who'd made her knees weak with his flashing smiles and silky voice?

Thinking to put him at ease, Maddie gently bumped her shoulder into his. "Thanks again for helping me out last night."

Eyes the color of a warm brownie searched her face as though seeking an answer to a question he hadn't asked. "Glad to."

He turned away from her again as though he hadn't just done something incredibly strange to her insides. Clearly, she didn't have any sort of effect on this man. Not like he had on her.

In fact, he seemed like he wanted nothing to do with her. Had she done something to offend him? Baffled, Maddie focused on her grandparents. The other side of the table fared nearly as badly. Sue Ellen looked out the window. Pops watched patrons at the bar. Neither seemed inclined to conversation.

"So…" Maddie plinked a fingernail on her Coke bottle. "What are you guys up to today?"

Catching sight of the waitress, Pops flagged her over. "Just two GIs with a little free time to spare."

*Thanks, Pops. Cleared that right up. What happened to "specifics are the key to communication"?*

She guessed Pops hadn't learned that gem yet.

The men discussed what they wanted to eat while the young waitress held her pen over her writing pad. Pops told Nate something about the cheese sauce. Apparently, that really was a thing around here. Finally, they decided on a pie filled with a half-dozen meats and toppings, and the waitress bounded off again, her ponytail flopping.

"What do you girls do when you're not hanging around the O club?" Pops asked.

Uh-oh. Maddie didn't do anything—at least not that she knew of—other than randomly show up in an apartment that she hadn't actually leased.

"I work at the club," Sue Ellen supplied. "In the kitchen mostly, but I also help waitress and occasionally run errands or do a little secretarial work for Mrs. Howard."

Pops lifted a brow. Maddie had forgotten how handsome he'd been. How could Nana not immediately fall for a guy like that?

"I haven't seen you there before."

Sue Ellen lifted the corner of her mouth. "Maybe you just never noticed."

Banter. Good. Maddie relaxed a little in her seat. Until Pops turned his gaze onto her.

"What about you, Miss Palmer?"

"I'm a music teacher." The words popped out of her mouth before she could stop them. She never had been good at lying. She got too flustered thinking she'd get caught, which of course always led to her getting caught.

Pops nodded as if that made perfect sense to him. But then, why wouldn't it? He didn't know she'd materialized out of thin air yesterday. The first pizza arrived a few moments later, along with a bottle of something orange. Maddie eyed the liquid. Surely that wasn't what Nana had called the cheese sauce. She wrinkled her nose but kept her opinion to herself.

Remembering the manners Nana would instill into her in a few decades, Maddie didn't bother to reach for their pizza even though her stomach rumbled. Polite people waited until everyone had been served before eating. The tantalizing scent of pepperoni tickled her senses.

Her tablemates talked about last night's dance, the music, and their favorite bands. Mostly, Maddie just listened as Nana and Pops hit it off. The more they laughed, the better she felt about this entire thing. The guys' pizza arrived a few moments later, and Pops immediately served the women from their pie before taking a slice of his own.

Nate scooped a piece so heavy with gooey cheese the end dipped. He plopped the greasy slice onto his plate and cast a glance around the table. "Mind if I ask a blessing?"

A Christian too? Maddie groaned to herself. *Why, God? Why wave a good-looking, God-honoring man I can never have right under my nose? Did You make a mistake and have me born in the wrong decade?*

A spark of excitement lit in her veins, but she doused it. Ridiculous. No matter how perfect the man beside her seemed, she wasn't here for him. Best she remember that before she ended up doing anything stupid. Maddie bowed her head.

Nate said a nice prayer that Maddie didn't really hear over her own weird conversation with the Creator.

*Why not point me to a man like that at home? Or do You mean to show me that the reason I can't find what I'm looking for is because all the men who are my type live in the past? Are You showing me that I'm always going to be single?*

Everyone said "amen," and Maddie snatched her focus back to the present—relatively speaking. Sue Ellen grabbed the bottle of orange sauce and squirted a generous amount over her slice of pizza. Maddie made a face she must have noticed.

"You have to try it. It's all the rage."

As she'd already said. But that was totally *not* cheese. "Um, not to be rude or anything, but are you sure that's cheese?"

Pops laughed and took the bottle. "It's a French-style dressing. I don't know why a bunch of kids started calling it cheese sauce, but the name stuck."

That made a lot more sense. Everyone looked at Maddie, so she caved to the pressure and squirted a tiny amount on the tip of her slice. She'd try a bite. No sense ruining an entire slice. She cocked her head at Nate.

"Are you going to try it?"

He shrugged. "Why not?" He scooped the bottle from her hand and doused his slice.

French dressing on pizza was a Biloxi tradition Nathanial had known his entire life. The trend had originated here at Hugo's and had become a Gulf Coast staple cemented into local culture during the fifties and sixties. Every time he'd eaten Gulf Coast pizza with his grandfather, they'd practically painted their slices with the stuff.

He didn't exactly love the combination, but he didn't hate it either. Besides, things like this reminded him of his family. Traditions were meant to be honored. And Nathanial never did anything halfway. If he committed to something, then he brought it all the way home.

Maddie looked at him like he'd lost his marbles as he finished slathering his toppings in dressing. Her eyes darted from his face to his food as though trying to understand if he actually meant to eat what was on his plate.

This woman had no problem openly staring. There was an honesty in her face that intrigued him. She seemed to be a person who never bothered trying to hide her true thoughts. Those wide eyes watched him, as though determined she'd witness him try the dressing before she would. He withheld a chuckle and took a big bite.

He smiled and nodded toward her waiting slice. She scrunched her nose, giving her round face a sprite-like look. She took a dainty bite and then shook her head.

"Nope." She wiped her lips with her napkin. "French dressing definitely does *not* belong on pepperoni."

She spoke with humor rather than disgust, and he couldn't help but chuckle. At least she knew what she liked and wasn't afraid to tell anyone. Or worry about fitting in with the others, who thought she should give it a fair chance. Maddie shook her head, decision made.

Nathanial glanced at the man across from him. Did her knowing exactly what she wanted include the major? She had been intently focused on the man last night.

Today, she kept cutting glances between the officer and her friend. Perhaps he'd been wrong and she actually hoped Mac would take an interest in the other woman. For some strange reason, the idea sparked a flame in his middle.

"How are you ladies spending this sunny afternoon?" Pops asked after wiping his mouth with a napkin.

Maddie looked to Sue Ellen, and the other woman shrugged. Maddie shot her a look that Nathanial guessed meant something. Women always did that. Speaking without words.

"We aren't sure yet," Maddie said, drawing the words out in a curious way. She looked at Sue Ellen again, who seemed overly interested in her pizza. "We're open to whatever the day may bring."

The suggestion in her tone painfully clear, Mac caught Nathanial's eye, asking a wordless question of his own. Should they invite the girls to spend the afternoon with them? He gave a small lift of his shoulder in silent response. He couldn't let it matter to him, regardless how Maddie stirred up his curiosity.

He had two objectives on this unforeseen mission. Figure out how to save Mac from flying into a hurricane and, in the meantime, find his grandfather and finally have a chance to say good-bye.

Women couldn't be part of his flight plan. Even a nearly irresistibly intriguing woman like Maddie.

# Nine

Maybe she hadn't made a mess of things after all. Nana and Pops strolled down the beach, shoes in their hands, engaged in conversation. Relief warmed her insides as the ocean breeze played with her hair.

All the same, she should probably get home before she caused any more glitches. Beside her, Nate strolled with his hands in his pockets, shoes tied at the laces and strung over his shoulder. In all honesty, she'd been surprised he'd tagged along. He didn't seem interested in spending the afternoon at the beach.

"Thanks again for helping me last night."

Nate nodded. "Sure."

So much for conversation. Why even bother?

"What's your history with Mac?"

The question surprised her. "Who?"

Nate turned to her, his face scrunched in confusion. He gestured ahead.

Duh. "Sorry. I don't know him by that name. I guess only his flight buddies call him that." Stupid.

Talking about Pops was bound to either get her into a tangle of lies or make her sound like she was a few notes short of a full song.

They walked a few paces more, Nate obviously waiting for her to answer an impossibly odd question.

"I don't really know him," she finally said. "But my friend does."

Nate's eyebrows dipped together. Maddie twisted her hands. Why did displeasing Nate cause such a sinking feeling in her stomach?

"I mean, she only met him yesterday, but they seemed to hit it off. They danced a lot last night. They make a lovely couple, don't you think?" She was rambling again. She did that when she got nervous, and Nate made her nervous. Enough that words tumbled out of her mouth in a disharmonious jumble.

"But they just met?"

She inwardly cringed. *Lord, how do I answer without lying?* "Yes."

Nate eyed her. "You said last night you were looking for an old friend. Then you saw Mac."

Had she? "I, uh, wanted him and Nan—um, I wanted him and Sue Ellen to dance. I knew they would hit it off."

Suspicion lit in his eyes, and he watched her, something calculating in the gaze. "Where do you teach music?"

"Before I came here, I taught at an academy in

Madison." Still the truth.

"And when did you move here?"

What was with the third degree? "Why do you ask?"

He sighed. "Sorry. Just making conversation."

Was he? Seemed like there had been something deeper lurking under his questions. She decided to turn the tables. "What about you? Where were you before coming here?"

"Stationed at Sheppard Air Force Base in Texas."

"What brought you to Biloxi?" Maddie sidestepped a wad of seaweed. Nana and Pops had drifted farther away, so she increased her speed.

"Training."

His face contorted in a strange way, and she had a feeling he was withholding information. But she could hardly pry without inviting the same. Shifting the subject to something more pleasant, she asked, "You're a Sinatra fan?"

Nate latched onto the switch, and his frown softened. "As are you, I take it."

Relaxing, Maddie laughed. "The classics are just so much more—" She stopped short as she realized her mistake. Stupid! Those weren't classics here.

Nate jerked to a halt. "What did you say?"

She barked a nervous laugh that sounded more like a frightened squirrel than she cared to admit. "I said those songs are more classy." Good save, right?

But a lie.

What did she do now? She couldn't tell this man the truth. But she didn't want to lie, either. She'd promised herself she'd never be like her mother. Would never hurt people with shiny lies to hide the rust underneath. But she'd landed in an impossible situation. The truth made her seem crazy, and the lies made her look like an idiot.

Lose-lose.

Nate studied her a moment, then continued walking. Maddie sucked in a gulp of salty air and followed. She must seem like a dimwit.

After a few moments, Nate picked up the conversation again as if she hadn't made a fool of herself. "What are your thoughts on Elvis?"

"Not really my style." Whew. A topic she could discuss truthfully. "Though I know a lot of people love him."

"Heard he has a girlfriend here in Biloxi. Is that true?"

Maddie searched her memory. "I think so."

A gull squawked overhead and swooped toward the water. Maddie watched its white wings glide through the air. She'd always loved the ocean. There was something peaceful about the gentle rhythm of the waves.

They walked quietly a little longer. How far would they wander down the beach? Since Nana and Pops seemed to be laughing and having a grand time, she would walk as far as they wanted to go.

"He's not my favorite either, though I do like a couple of his songs," Nate said.

"Which ones?"

Nate hesitated a moment. "'Jailhouse Rock' is pretty good."

Huh. She thought "Jailhouse Rock" had been a later song. But obviously not. "Not familiar with that one."

Another lie.

Maybe she should start thinking of herself as an actress in a play. Then she wouldn't exactly be lying, she'd only be playing a part. The thought shifted some weight off her shoulders. But it came crashing back down almost immediately. Was that the type of person she wanted to be? She'd promised herself she would always be honest, and here she was making excuses for lies by justifying their necessity.

Had her mother done the same those times she'd called and told Maddie she'd come home for good soon but never did? Did Mom think that justifying the lie would somehow help? The thought left a bitter taste in her mouth. A pretty lie was still a lie. And finding out the truth later only brought more pain.

No. She'd find a way to be truthful and not give herself away. Or maybe she'd just tell everyone she'd teleported from the twenty-first century to the past and see how they handled the idea. The problem with that was that she wouldn't be able to get back to the inn if someone threw her in the nuthouse.

Too many decisions. She'd think about that later.

Instead, she focused on the sights around her. The scent of the briny ocean, the call of the gulls.

In the distance, the late afternoon sun shown on a large sign with a lighthouse shape on one end.

Pops paused in the sand and waited for them to catch up. He gestured toward the lighthouse, which Maddie could now see was a sign for a seaside drive-in movie theatre. "Sue Ellen and I are going to watch the show tonight. You two want to join us?"

"Yes!" Maddie blurted before she could stop herself. She glanced at Nate, who surely had to think she'd been overly eager to go out with him. Heat rose in her cheeks.

Nate chuckled. "Y'all have fun. Think I should head back to the barracks."

Pops glanced between them and gave a nod while Nana gave Maddie a sympathetic smile. This had to look awful. Like she was head over heels for Nate and he didn't have the slightest sliver of interest in her. She avoided his gaze.

"Bus stop's just ahead," Pops said. "We'll walk you girls there." He checked his watch and smiled at Sue Ellen. "Meet you here at eight?"

Nana pulled her lower lip between her teeth. Uh-oh. She was about to refuse. Stupid Nate. Why couldn't he have just played along? Nana wouldn't want to leave her out or deal with a third wheel and then she would tell

Pops no and—

"Sure."

Huh. Sue Ellen shot Maddie another apologetic look, but Maddie only smiled.

Something was off about that girl. He knew it. He'd tried prodding her a bit to see if he could find any evidence for his suspicion that she might not be as native to the 1950s as he'd first thought. But each time he caught her saying something off, she'd cover it up just as quickly. He couldn't decide if the woman was weird or hiding something.

Maybe he'd been looking for something that wasn't there. Looking for a shard of evidence that someone else had fallen down the rabbit hole. A thin hope that he wasn't alone.

He shook his head. He needed to stay focused.

"Regretting turning down a date with a pretty girl?"

Nathanial snapped his head up as they neared the major's car. "What? No. Just thinking."

"What's on your mind?"

Too many things he couldn't share. Except for maybe one thing. "I was thinking of trying to look up an old friend, but I'm not sure how to find him."

"Stationed here?"

"No." At least, he was pretty sure Granddad hadn't been at Keesler in the fifties. But he couldn't remember exactly.

They reached the car, and Mac popped open the door. "Live in Biloxi?"

Where had Granddad lived in fifty-six? He had no idea. "I don't know." He rounded the car and opened the passenger door.

Mac slid inside and cranked the engine. "I see your problem. Hard to find a man when you don't know where he lives." Mac chuckled, but the statement only formed a pit in Nathanial's stomach.

Maybe he wasn't meant to find his grandfather. He needed to focus on the task at hand, even if the lost opportunity panged him. The mission came first. The mission always came first.

Even when it cost him. Or when it caused him to hurt others.

The thought immediately brought a pang of guilt. Nathanial should have been there for his mother. Should have requested leave and stayed at her side. Instead, he'd been duty-bound to complete his assignment and had left her in the wake of her best friend's funeral to deal with the loss alone.

If the mission coming first had cost Mom pain, he couldn't very well forsake his mission now to sooth his own hurts. Hardly seemed right. Resigned, he set aside thoughts of finding his grandfather.

"Sure you don't want to join us tonight?" Mac asked.

"Probably better if I don't. No need to get involved with a girl."

Mac seemed to consider the statement as they paused at a red light. "Not interested in dating in general, or just Miss Palmer?"

He *was* interested in Miss Palmer. That was the problem. Forcing a change of subject, he looked for an opening into what mattered. "Sir, do you mind if I have a look at your bird? I'm interested in what kind of equipment you have on board."

Mac eyed him a second. "Should be able to get an instructor clearance to the flight line. But she's pretty standard."

"Thank you, sir. I'd appreciate it."

Mac eyed him again but kept whatever opinion swam behind his eyes to himself.

They drove the rest of the way back to the base in silence, and Mac stopped at temporary lodging. After hopping out, Nathanial leaned down and looked in the window. "Lunch was good, sir. Thanks for the invite."

Mac grinned. "Anytime. See you around."

Nathanial watched the man drive off. Good fellow. And he seemed to be interested in Sue Ellen. Would they have had a future together? Had they already lived a happy life?

He pulled open the front door and stepped into the

lobby, a weight slung around his shoulders. Focus on the mission. No more getting sidetracked. He had to figure out how to rewrite history.

Time to formulate a plan. Starting with how to break into a mysterious bed and breakfast.

# Ten

He probably should turn back. Forget this stupid idea. The last thing he needed was to get himself thrown into jail. The police would ask too many questions. Still, Nathanial walked with a purpose down the seaside road toward The Depot.

The hurricane would be only a few days away. The storm would soon smash through an oil rig and steal the lives of the entire crew of the Magnolia Mayhem.

And he intended to save them. Somehow.

That started with The Depot. Primarily because he had no idea what else to do. If the old Victorian remained timeless, then maybe his history books were there. Even better, maybe he could use his phone. The internet. Who knew how worm holes worked? Despite what Mrs. Easley said, maybe he could go inside and right back to the present.

Maybe that's why Mrs. Easley had locked him out.

Without bothering to climb the steps to the front porch, Nathanial continued around the flowering bushes and to the rear of the house. Another porch greeted him.

Sweat broke out on the back of his neck. Did he really plan on breaking and entering? Not *breaking*. Not if he could help it. He tried the backdoor knob. Locked. As he had suspected.

But older people often lost their keys, didn't they? Where would Mrs. Easley hide a spare?

He studied the space. A pair of rocking chairs and a shared end table. Lots of potted plants. He tried the plants first. The smaller ones revealed nothing underneath. He doubted Mrs. Easley would attempt to lift the larger ones, but he tried them anyway.

Nothing.

A small ceramic turtle caught his attention. Nestled at the base of a plant with big pink flowers, the little turtle's shell was nearly hidden in the foliage. He grabbed the shell to lift the turtle and check underneath its body, but the shell itself came off in his hand.

Bingo.

A shiny silver key sat on the turtle's back. He plucked the key from its hiding place and replaced the ceramic shell. The key turned easily in the doorknob.

He hesitated. Did she have an alarm? Not that he remembered, but then why would he have been looking for an alarm system? Throwing a quick prayer for favor heavenward, he pushed open the door.

Nothing happened.

He let out a sigh of relief and stepped into the kitchen. He didn't feel anything weird. No warning pulses of light or strange tingles to let him know he'd time-jumped. He closed the door, then swept it open again. Nothing outside had changed.

But how would he know if anything had? The Depot had looked exactly the same when he'd woken up in the past. There'd be no way to know until he headed down the street again.

He passed through the kitchen and dining room and then out to the main hallway. No changes that he could tell here either. The flowers on the table in the hall were still fresh.

Had Mrs. Easley lied to him? Was she still here somewhere? He stepped cautiously. Being caught sneaking through the house wouldn't be good.

But then again, he'd paid for a room here and had used a key to enter. He straightened. He had every right. His belongings were here, after all. Nathanial tromped up the stairs, less concerned with making noise.

The pictures he'd never really noticed on the wall caught his attention. Boston Harbor, likely Revolutionary period. A Western wagon train. WWII planes. Paintings of different places. Different times. Curious, he continued past his room down the hall. A Scottish castle. Early Native Americans on a hillside with buffalo.

He paused. Rather than another painting, one particularly large frame held a photograph. A black-and-white of a young Mrs. Easley leaning against the sign for Keesler AFB. He leaned closer, squinting. Looking for time-travel clues.

Shaking his head at himself, he leaned back. So the woman had a picture of herself from the fifties hanging in her hallway. Nothing strange about that. And she liked paintings from different times. Nothing suspicious there.

Ignoring a nagging feeling that said there was more here than he cared to unearth, Nathanial hurried back down the hall to his room. The unlocked door swung open. Sunlight poured through the large windows, washing the room in cheery light.

Nathanial checked the armoire. His shoulders sagged. Nothing. Not his uniforms, his duffle bag, his Bible, or even his shoes sat inside. The bathroom didn't hold any of his toiletries.

He withheld a groan. So much for finding any of his stuff. Looked like he'd be stuck with the basics in temporary housing. Probably should make a BX run and grab a few more items to hold him over until the hurricane passed. He checked the drawers just in case, but as he expected, didn't find anything.

On the writing desk, however, sat his class manual. It had been left opened to the very page that detailed the history of Hurricane Flossy. A weird sensation tingled at the back of his neck as he sat at the desk.

*Hurricane Flossy moved into the Gulf of Mexico as a tropical depression on September 21, 1956 and became a tropical storm on September 22 and a hurricane on September 23.*

What was today? He'd arrived on the fourteenth. That made today Saturday the fifteenth. The storm would enter the Gulf this Friday. He quickly scanned the information, looking for what mattered the most.

*Unknown in-flight complications cost the lives of the five-man crew on the WB-29 "Magnolia Mayhem" of the 27th Weather Reconnaissance Squadron. The pilot, Major Robert MacBride, and his crew flew into the eyewall at an altitude of 700 feet.*

They entered at seven hundred feet? Hurricane winds were far too unpredictable at that altitude. The last transmission from the crew had come before they'd entered the eyewall, and they hadn't given any indications of trouble. No more transmissions had been received after they'd penetrated the center of the storm.

They were never heard from again, the plane never recovered.

Nathanial sat back. Why did MacBride fly that low? Engine problems? Miscalculations? Nathanial wasn't a mechanic. The best he could do was put eyes on the plane before she flew out.

But if it had something to do with meteorology

observations or avionics, then he had one other option.

Fly with them into the storm.

Maddie dusted her dress off and watched the bus pull away from the curb. Time to go home. She'd stayed an extra day, but now that Nana and Pops had plans for their first date, she felt sure they'd be fine. She'd seen their romance unfold. From here it would be only a matter of days until Pops proposed. They'd marry in a whirlwind and live happily ever after. They didn't need her.

Besides, if she stayed any longer, she was more likely to mess something up.

Nana had been kind to invite her to join them at the drive-in tonight. She'd almost lied and said she had a headache but had decided on the truth instead. No one wanted a third wheel. Not the couple, and certainly not the spare tire.

Helping Nana with her hair, gushing like girlfriends, made her miss her grandmother, strange as that sounded. She walked down the tree-lined street, the scents of flowers and ocean air intoxicating. She wasn't meant to stay here. She should be at Nana and Pops's party.

Even if time played out the same, then she should

still arrive Saturday afternoon. Right in the middle of the party. Nana would be disappointed she'd missed early morning coffee, but she'd make the anniversary celebration.

Hopefully, she'd go back to the present exactly when she'd left. But since she couldn't remember how she got from her room at The Depot to the apartment, who knew what would happen?

The house hadn't moved, so she figured the best way to get home was simply to go back to the B&B. Maybe as soon as she went inside, she'd end up back in her own time.

She neared the house and glanced at the carved wooden sign.

*Step back "inn" time and leave your troubles behind.*

Maddie rolled her eyes. Who would have ever thought to take that sign literally? She walked up the steps and hesitated on the wide porch. Did she just go in?

Obviously, the house took guests. Even if she waltzed in, she wouldn't be entering someone's home unannounced. She tried the knob. Locked.

She knocked on the door and stepped back to wait. There were no cars in the driveway. Maybe no one was home. She knocked again.

Footsteps? She leaned closer to listen, then breathed a sigh of relief. Someone was coming down the stairs.

Maddie stepped back and squared her shoulders. Would she be greeted by the same woman she'd met before?

No, that was silly. But then again, maybe not. Maybe this house existed in some kind of time-warp bubble. Mrs. Easley would look exactly the same. She'd greet Maddie, and Maddie would go to her room. Find her things. Gather her luggage, check out. Step outside back in the future and make a beeline to Nana and Pops's house.

Never to return to this place again.

A shadow moved across one of the windows flanking the front door, then quickly disappeared. Maddie frowned. Someone was inside but hadn't come to the door. Maybe they hadn't heard her. She knocked again, nearly pounding this time.

No way whoever it was hadn't heard that. She waited again, but no one came.

Weird.

She whirled around and headed down the front steps. Skirting some hydrangeas, Maddie marched up the driveway and to the detached garage. Maybe whoever had been inside would be heading to their car.

The garage door stood closed. She peeked through the dusty glass but saw nothing inside but a few gardening supplies. No car. None parked anywhere around.

Maybe she'd try the back door. A thought skittered through her mind that maybe whoever was inside wouldn't take kindly to company, but she dismissed the idea. This house was still an inn, not a private residence. The sign outside proved as much.

Probably a guest who didn't think they should open the door, seeing as how such things would be left to the owner. Telling herself that had to be the case, she passed through a small gate into the neatly manicured backyard. Like a miniature garden meant for afternoon teas, the landscaping called a person to sit a spell and relax.

But Maddie didn't have time for that. She marched up the rear steps and onto the picturesque back porch. Rocking chairs and a variety of potted plants graced the space. Barely giving them a glance, she knocked sharply on the back door.

No answer.

She tried the knob. This one turned easily. She stepped inside. "Hello? Anyone here?"

Moving from room to room, Maddie made her way through the lower floor, looking for Mrs. Easley. No one answered her greeting.

Must have been a guest who didn't answer the door and who'd then slipped out the back before she came around. And then left. Without a car.

A shiver she tried to ignore ran down her spine. So weird.

But nothing about any of this was normal. She walked upstairs and to her room, pleased to find her door unlocked. She paused inside the doorway, the breath of relief sticking in her throat. Her suitcase was gone.

She groaned. Maybe her stuff had stayed in the future? Sure. Why wouldn't that be the case? Except, she'd been hoping she'd already passed back into the future as soon as she'd entered the wormhole house. Obviously not. The time travel had to be triggered another way.

What had happened that night? Retracing her steps, she pretended to pull her suitcase into the room. The mirror. How had she forgotten about the super-strange mirror that had showed her dressed in an entirely different outfit?

Hadn't the surface shimmered? The mirror had to be the key.

Stepping up to it, she studied her reflection. Her normal face stared back at her. She wore the right clothes this time. Maybe seeing herself dressed differently in the reflection had been a dream. She reached out and touched the mirror.

Her reflection did the same.

Nothing happened.

# Eleven

*M*addie's heart fluttered. Would she be stuck here forever? She tried the mirror again, with the same result. What now?

Mrs. Easley. Where had the woman gone? She had to know something. Maddie hurried to the kitchen and found a notepad and pen by the refrigerator. She paused and stared at the appliance. Had this been the same one here in the future? Who could tell? Everything in this house was a hodgepodge of antiques. The rounded edges looked like something from the fifties, but that didn't mean much.

She grabbed a pen. Best she could do was leave a note. Good thing there'd been an information card in the apartment with the phone number and address along with the landlord's contact information. She'd always been good with numbers and had memorized the seven digits easily.

After writing a quick note to Mrs. Easley asking the woman to please call her apartment at the first available opportunity, Maddie stepped back outside.

What if Mrs. Easley didn't find the note? What if she didn't exist in this time?

No sense scrambling her brain with too many questions. She pulled the door closed behind her and drew several long breaths. She needed to think. Make a plan. Returning to the house and touching the mirror hadn't sent her back to her time. So what now? Sleeping hadn't worked either. She'd slept after the dance and hadn't woken up in the future.

Maybe she really had been sent here permanently. But why? Would something have happened to her in the future? But what would her grandparents think?

What about her mom? Would she care if Maddie never came back?

Maddie pushed the thought away. She couldn't do anything about her situation anyway. She couldn't *will* herself back to the future.

Could she?

Pausing in the rear garden, Maddie glanced around to see if anyone was watching her. Alone, she squeezed her eyes shut and thought like Dorothy.

"There's no place like home," she whispered.

She opened her eyes, finding everything the same. As if wishing would work. As if wishing ever worked. If it had, she'd have found a man to share her life with. Or her mother never would have left. Sighing, Maddie latched the gate and rounded the house. Better head back before she missed the bus. The street looked much the same as Maddie remembered, minus a few important houses. Like Nana's.

Cars passed, many blaring lively jukebox tunes from open windows. The breeze played with her hair as she walked, sending strands across her nose. A sense of loneliness wrapped cold fingers around her heart and squeezed, but she pointedly ignored the feeling.

Drawing herself out of her contemplations about time travel and starting a new life here, her eyes snagged the bus.

Oh no.

She bolted forward, scrambling down the sidewalk. The wheels started to roll, and the driver signaled the vehicle would soon merge into traffic.

Maddie sprinted forward and reached the door just as the two sections folded closed. "Wait!" She pounded on the small window at eye level.

The startled driver paused, blinked, and finally thrust open the door.

Maddie scrambled inside and dropped her money in the can mounted at the dash. "Whew. Thanks!"

The man didn't even acknowledge her. Goodness, the bus was full. One seat near the middle remained open. She hurried down the aisle as they swayed into traffic and dropped into the seat with an undignified plop.

The person beside her chuckled. Dressed in a

stained shirt she guessed had once been a white tee, the young man had his sandy hair slicked back with what had to be an entire tub of pomade. Maddie smiled. Perhaps movies like *Grease* weren't as far-fetched as she'd first thought. This boy looked as if he'd stepped right off the set. Down to his cuffed sleeves and the pack of cigarettes in his pocket.

"What's got you all in a rush, missy?"

Maddie blew a breath up her face. "Almost missed the bus."

He grinned. "Good thing you made it. Else we'd never have met." His gaze dipped down over her. "Name's George Fisher."

A feeling—that same one that had risen like bile on more than one of her disastrous dates—twisted in her stomach. She tried to scoot to the edge of the seat without him noticing. She gave a polite nod. "Nice to meet you, George." She turned her eyes forward and leaned into the aisle, looking out the windshield.

"Not going to give me your name, missy?"

Maddie gave the guy an assessing look. Upon closer examination, he couldn't be out of high school. Boys that age had too much bravado and too little sense. She gave him the type of smile she gave her students. Friendly, but no-nonsense.

"Miss Palmer."

He scooted a little closer. "Where you headed?"

Away from him, if possible. Maddie leaned farther

away and narrowed her eyes. "Home." She kept the word curt, but the boy didn't seem to take the hint. He smiled at her, a gleam in his blue eyes.

Ugh. What was it about her that drew creeps like flies to honey? "Excuse me, Mr. Fisher, but you're leaning into my seat."

His gaze raked down her. "Then how about you scoot in, and I won't have to lean so far?"

"How about you leave the lady alone before you and I have a problem?" a smooth masculine voice intervened.

Maddie looked up at the sound, and her heart somersaulted.

Nate.

The grungy kid scowled at him. "This ain't none of your concern."

The muscles in Nathanial's jaw clenched. He looked at Maddie, who had gone pale. "Why don't you take my seat?" He nodded toward the back. "And I'll sit here."

The boy's eyes widened as Maddie lurched to her feet. The driver shouted for them to sit down, but Nathanial didn't care. People were staring at them now. Heads turned toward him, necks straining to get a good look.

He ignored them. He wouldn't let her be harassed no matter how many people stared.

Maddie ducked her head and hurried toward the back. Nathanial lowered himself into her vacated seat, earning a glower from the boy. He could hardly be called a man. This kid was exactly the type who could use the military life. Enlistment would zap that attitude right out of him. Make something more substantial out of all that pent-up energy.

Like the Air Force had done for him.

Remembering the kid he'd been, Nathanial relaxed a little. "Name's Captain Hall." He held out his hand.

The greaser stared at Nathanial's outstretched hand for a moment but then begrudgingly offered a firm shake. "George Fisher."

Nathanial smiled. Might be hope for the kid after all.

"That your girl?" George asked.

Nathanial shook his head. "Just a friend."

George's forehead crinkled in confusion. "You sure acted like you had a claim on her." Defensiveness rose in his tone.

"I look out for my friends. You were making her uncomfortable."

George mumbled something impolite under his breath.

Granddad would say that the boy could use a lesson in manners. "Ever think about joining the military?"

"No way." George huffed and turned his face to the window. "Don't want to turn into some meathead who thinks he can bully another man away from a pretty broad."

"Maddie Palmer isn't some broad," Nathanial snapped. "And she isn't the type to take a second look at the likes of you."

As soon as the words left his mouth, he regretted them. What did he know about Maddie Palmer? Very little other than the way her eyes lit up when she sang, that she loved Sinatra, and that she had an undeniable *something* that pulled him to her the way wind was sucked into an engine turbine.

But she'd seemed uncomfortable when he'd spotted her leaning into the middle of the aisle, and that had been enough to propel him from his seat. He hadn't even thought before taking action. Him, the man who usually considered every option before jumping into motion.

What was it about that woman that got to him?

He leaned back in his seat, contemplating. The guy at his side remained in sullen silence. The bus pulled off at the stop they'd taken for pizza earlier, and a flash of pink fabric scurried down the aisle. Maddie?

Why was she getting off here? The way she moved concerned him. All jittery, like a butterfly frantically fighting against a windstorm. Was something wrong?

Before he could convince himself that whatever

agitated her was none of his business, he was on his feet and following.

George Fisher made a snide comment Nathanial chose to ignore as he waited for three other people to exit between him and Maddie. On the street, people languidly strolled the sidewalks, enjoying the pleasant Saturday evening. He rose on his toes and located the head of glossy brown hair.

He jogged to her side. When he reached her, Maddie yelped, turning to face him with a start. "Oh!"

"Sorry. Didn't mean to startle you." He rocked back on his heels when she didn't reply. "Are you all right? After the bus, I mean."

She continued to assess him, making him feel almost as dressed down as a skittish new recruit under the withering gaze of a cantankerous drill sergeant.

"Is this your stop?"

It took a moment for her meaning to register. "I was headed to the base."

"But you got off here instead."

All he could do was nod awkwardly and stand there like an idiot. No sense trying to explain why he'd followed her off the bus, seeing as he didn't actually have an explanation.

What had she been doing on that bus anyway? She'd gotten on at the same stop he had. The last one before The Depot. She couldn't have been the person knocking on the B&B door that he'd narrowly avoided.

Could she?

She pursed her lips, then as though deciding something for herself, bobbed her head. "Thanks for switching seats."

People streamed around them, ducking into seaside shops and restaurants. He edged a little closer to Maddie, trying to get out of the middle of the sidewalk. "Can I walk you to wherever you're headed?"

Her eyebrows pulled together. Maybe she didn't want his company. Or she had somewhere to go she didn't want him following. Suspicion wormed through his veins. Maybe she had been at the weird Victorian house. Did she know something he didn't?

She was eyeing him as skeptically as he'd been eyeing her. "I thought you had plans for this evening." Something in her tone had seemed almost...snippy.

Realization slammed into him. Oh. He'd turned down the invitation to the drive-in movie tonight. Which, he could see now, had likely embarrassed Maddie after her excitement to go. He was an idiot.

Here he was suspecting her of secretly visiting the inn when she'd been thinking about the callous way he'd turned down an evening in her company. No wonder she'd been skeptical of him wanting to walk with her.

He kneaded the muscles in the back of his neck. This was probably why he stayed away from women. He was too rough around the edges and too thickheaded where other people's feelings were concerned. "Sorry about that."

She watched him, eyes seeming to read him.

Nathanial sighed. He was botching up his attempt at mending what he'd broken the last time he botched things up. "I didn't mean to be rude to you, Maddie. I promise. I had planned on going back to the base, but then I had some other business to take care of and well…" He shrugged. The excuse sounded terrible.

She probably thought he was a total jerk.

She lifted her chin and glanced around him, clearly wishing to remove herself from his company. He should let her go. Leave her alone, as he'd originally planned. But then, if he ended up spending the rest of his life in the past, what would it hurt to get to know her?

He had no control over his future. No say in where he ended up. He only had today. This moment. And for once in his life, he was going to live in the moment presented.

"I'm really sorry about earlier," he said, holding her gaze and hoping she could see his sincerity. "When Mac asked about the movies. I see now how my response seemed like I didn't want your company and therefore turned down what would have been a date with you. My mind was elsewhere, and I admit I wondered if I should let myself get distracted by you."

Her eyes widened.

"I've also realized, however, that you are a most fascinating distraction—and one I would welcome."

Maddie stared at him, looking as surprised by his statement as he felt. When had he ever been so direct with his thoughts to a woman? Probably never, save his interactions with his mother and sister. And expressing his feelings to them was nothing like doing so with Maddie. He shifted his feet, unused to the nerves making him sweat.

He could handle a barrel roll in a plane at Mach 1, and his stomach felt steadier at ten thousand feet than the quivering he sustained under her gaze. What was wrong with him?

She blinked a couple of times and then gave him a charming smile. "Is that so? Well, what if I find I shouldn't be distracted by you either, Captain?"

He grinned, tension rolling off at her teasing tone. "Then I say the two of us will be in good company. Both enjoying the non-distracting manner of the other. So as to avoid a conundrum, of course."

Maddie threw her head back and laughed, and he didn't know if he'd ever heard a more enticing sound. He offered his arm as he thought a fifties man might do. She eyed him a moment, then slipped her hand through the crook of his elbow. Her touch lit something deep inside him.

They stood there awkwardly for a moment as Nathanial realized he was supposed to lead but had no idea where she'd been going. "Uh, where are we headed?"

"I have no idea."

What? "You didn't know where you were going when you got off at this stop?"

She shook her head. "Stupid, I know. But I wasn't ready to go home yet. Thought I'd see the town instead of sitting alone in my apartment."

He cringed. "Well then, how about we take a stroll?"

She smiled, but it quickly faltered. "You don't have something better to do?"

Nope. Looking down at her beautiful face and questioning eyes, he couldn't think of anywhere in the world he'd rather be than walking with her on his arm.

# Twelve

She shouldn't be doing this, walking on the arm of a man who would most assuredly break her heart. Even if he didn't mean to. She could be swept away at any moment, never to see him again.

Except maybe as an old man. Maybe even a buddy of her grandfather's.

And yet she couldn't help herself. Couldn't stop herself from smiling. People milled on the sidewalks, a sense of peace and openness filling the streets with them. Maybe she was vicariously nostalgic and saw this time as Nana had always described it. Or maybe an air of joy really did fill this post-war era.

And then again, maybe her sense that all was right with the world came entirely from the handsome pillar of manliness next to her.

Nate was charming, funny, not to mention nice to look at. Everything a girl wanted all packaged up in the wrong time.

But if she wasn't going home, then maybe he wasn't

so wrong after all. Her grip tightened on his arm as they walked. She didn't know. Had no idea what tomorrow would bring. Time travel had a way of forcing perspective.

Deep inside, she'd always known she'd never really had control over what the world threw at her, though she always planned as though she did. Paralyzed herself in indecision most of the time for fear of making the wrong choice or of somehow making a mess of everything.

Now, she was forced to see her life in moment-by-moment pieces. Why worry over what the next minute might bring? She could zap back to the future at any second. Or get hit by a bus. She glanced at Nate. Or fall off a cliff into some very powerful emotions. Who knew?

She simply needed to live in the present. Relatively speaking.

"Want to head over to the beach, or are you hungry?" Nate's voice drew her from her thoughts.

"Beach sounds nice." Sunset on the beach? Talk about romantic.

He led her across the road at the crosswalk and down to the public access point. They removed their shoes for the second time that day and let their toes caress the sand.

Maddie drew a deep breath. "I've always loved the ocean." The way the balmy breeze danced across her face. The feel of warm sand on the bottom of her feet.

As Nate stared at the gentle waves, she sensed his agreement. They walked down to the water's edge, and he looked around, eyes searching. "Do you mind sitting on the sand, or should we go back up to find a bench?"

She laughed and plopped down, stretching out her legs. "Here works."

His slow smile sent a flutter through her. He settled next to her and rested his forearms on his knees. The water lapped gently beyond their toes, far enough away that she didn't have to fear a stray wave might leave her soaked.

"What are your plans for the future?" Nate asked, still staring out at the water.

Way to skip the small talk. On every date she'd been on, they'd discussed mundane things. What they each did at work. How many siblings they had. No one had ever asked her something that seemed to probe right past all the useless, surface-level talk people usually engaged in. She found that interesting. A product of the time, or the man himself?

"I'm not sure I really have any," she responded honestly. "I thought I had a few things mapped out, but life seems to have a way of meddling with my plans."

He laughed. "I know exactly how you feel."

"What about you?"

"Finish training, request assignment with the Hurricane Hunters, get stationed at Keesler. Maybe buy a house. Get a dog."

Wow. All that was missing from that sentence was "find a wife." Instead of letting herself go down that path, Maddie focused on the other part of what he'd said. "Hurricane Hunters?"

He looked at her curiously, as though she should know what that meant. "They are a reconnaissance division. Fly into the storms and collect data. Helps to give a more accurate forecast. Saves lives."

Said with such conviction. "Sounds dangerous."

"No more dangerous than any other job, really. At least this way, you know you're flying out to meet trouble rather than being blindsided when it finds you instead."

"Have you ever been blindsided by trouble?" she asked, picking up on a deeper meaning to his words.

Nate laced his fingers together and watched the sun dip lower toward the water. He took his time in answering, but when he did, his voice remained calm, if not somewhat hard. "My dad was a police officer. Routine traffic stop. Regular day. Except that day the guy in the car wasn't speeding. He was driving too slowly." His voice grew rougher. "He was strung out and running two kilos of heroin through our town. He pulled over. Then shot my dad as he approached."

Maddie's breath caught. How awful. She had no idea things like that happened in the—what—forties? Drug runners and kilos of heroin sounded like something from her time that didn't belong in the peaceful world here.

Something nagged in the back of her mind that there was more to this story, but she ignored it. She didn't want to miss sharing this vulnerable moment with him by letting herself slip into another one of her own internal debates.

She looped her hand through the crook of his elbow again and trailed her fingers down his forearm, searching for words of comfort that didn't come. When she reached his hand, he opened his palm, inviting her to stay. She slid her hand over his and laced her thin fingers between his larger ones.

"Dad dove behind the man's vehicle for cover," he said, squeezing her hand as he stared at their entwined fingers. "Probably expected the guy to speed off." The muscles in his jaw clenched. "The guy backed over him for good measure, in case the gunshot wound hadn't been enough." He shook his head. "Left my dad there on the side of the road in the middle of the night. By the time a passerby found him an hour later, there was nothing they could do."

Tears stung her eyes and she leaned into him. "I'm so sorry. That must have been awful."

He nodded.

"Did they catch him?"

"He's still sitting in prison. Life sentence." He stared out at the sunset, tension in his shoulders.

How could she only have just met this man and feel like they'd known each other for years? Feel like they could share their pasts, talk about their hopes and dreams?

She caressed the back of his hand with her thumb. "How old were you when that happened?"

"Thirteen. Times were hard. As soon as I was old enough, I enlisted to help take care of my mom and sister."

Throat dry, Maddie leaned her head on his shoulder. The raw sincerity of his story and the fact that he'd shared something so personal stirred her heart. They sat there for a time, watching the sun paint reds and oranges across a few white wispy clouds. Maybe the emotion of the moment, the sunset, or the fact that she didn't want to hold back and miss the time given to her made her illogical, but something in her heart cracked open and urged her to share as well.

She hadn't lost a parent in the way he had, but her heart also bore scars. Scars she thought she could share with Nate, scars she thought he would somehow understand.

"My mom decided when I was eleven that my dad and I weren't enough for her."

Nate cast her a quick glance, but she continued to stare out at the dipping sunset. The light painted the blue water in shades of purple. God's nightly artistry.

"One day mom decided she no longer wanted to

keep house and waste away in the middle of nowhere." Those words spoken by her mother at breakfast one morning had branded Maddie's young heart. Even after all these years, they still burned. "She said she needed to find herself. See the world. She did, I suppose. Found one man after another to take her on grand adventures. I kept thinking that once she'd seen enough, she'd realize she had a good man and a nice home waiting on her. But she never did."

Nate's arm slipped around her shoulders, and the warmth of him made her want to melt into his side.

"Sometimes she would call. Maybe whenever she felt guilty for abandoning me. She would promise that she'd be coming home soon. Eventually, I realized those were lies. Maybe they made her feel better. But all they did was make things worse for me. My dad finally divorced her when I was in the tenth grade. She came back then, but only to take what little the courts had granted her. I haven't seen her since."

Would her mother have gone to Nana and Pops's anniversary party? Seen her parents celebrate a marriage that had lasted decades? Probably not. Not after she'd thrown her own marriage away. She hadn't even come back when Dad died two years ago.

Nana and Pops were all Maddie had in this world. Her mother didn't count as family.

Nate squeezed her against him. "I'm sorry."

The simple words she'd heard so many times from

others rang with a new depth of sincerity. Almost like Nate hadn't said the words because they were expected but rather because he truly meant he was sorry for her pain. She turned to look at him. Clean shaven, masculine nose and chin.

He met her gaze, his nose nearly brushing hers. Her heart hammered. His eyes swam with something she couldn't name but held her captive. What would happen if she leaned in and kissed him? He'd think her bold. Maybe worse. Women in the fifties didn't do things like that, did they? They didn't just—

His head tilted. In slow motion his eyes dropped to half closed.

Her breath caught. He leaned in, just a little.

She touched the side of his face, lightly testing. Those eyes darkened, drawing her in. His arm tightened until the space between them no longer existed. His warm lips grazed hers. Gently, as though asking her permission.

Maddie leaned into him, increasing the pressure. Heat flooded through her, and she threaded her fingers into his hair, drawing him closer. He deepened the kiss, and she forgot all about watching the sunset.

Nate lost all sense of reservations. Maddie melted into

his arms, her lips soft and sweet beneath his. The woman intoxicated him, but rather than drawing back, he could only let himself sink deeper.

His fingers found the soft waterfall of her hair, and he pulled her even tighter against him. Something in him shifted. This woman affected him in the most illogical ways, but at the moment, he couldn't bring himself to care.

The scent of her flowery shampoo flooded his senses, and somewhere in the back of his mind, a little voice told him to regain his control. Reluctantly, he eased back and slowly softened the kiss until his lips whispered against hers.

She rested her forehead on his, eyes still closed. "Wow."

He chuckled. "My thoughts exactly."

They stared at one another a moment, and the force of the feelings that crashed through him made no sense. He hardly knew this woman, yet he already knew he'd do anything in his power to protect her. Probably try give her anything she desired.

She had some kind of power over him. More than attraction, more than physical yearning. He couldn't begin to decode what swirled like a hurricane in him, but whatever it was, he'd let the tempest sweep him away.

Life in the fifties suddenly got a whole lot more complicated.

"I think we missed the sunset." Her words came out more breath than anything, and he smiled.

His own voice rasped in his throat. "I'd gladly miss any sunset with you."

Her lips tilted into a cute smile, and he had the overwhelming temptation to taste them again. But if he didn't get a hold of himself, this current would drag him under. He forced himself to lean back a little out of her gravitational pull. "How about supper?"

She cocked an eyebrow. "Are you asking me out on a date, Mr. Hall?"

"I am." He chuckled. "That is, if you'd have one uptight, rather sandy airman as your escort." Where had *that* come from? What was this woman doing to him? He completely lost himself in her presence.

She made a mock gasp. "Why, that is precisely the kind of man I've been looking for." She winked. "Do you know any?"

Despite himself, he threw his head back and laughed. Maddie Palmer was one of a kind. He stood and helped her to her feet. They brushed off the sand and walked hand in hand back toward the road.

What would it be like to stay here? Date Maddie? If he did that, who would be there for his mother? What would she think if he never came home?

Like his father had never come home?

The thought tainted the perfect evening, so he forced himself to turn his mind elsewhere. A problem for another day. Who knew how long he would be here. One thing he knew for certain. He wouldn't miss a single moment he'd been granted with Maddie.

Not if he could help it.

# Thirteen

Maddie entered her apartment floating on clouds. At least, she suspected this was how floating might feel—as if her emotions carried her so high her feet barely brushed the floor. What a night. She closed the door behind her with a sigh.

"Where have you been?"

Nana's voice made Maddie yelp. "Oh! You scared the life out of me." She turned to look at the younger version of her grandmother standing in her robe with her hair in curlers.

Give her a few more wrinkles and some gray hair, and the woman looked exactly the same.

How weird. Nana's voice had made her feel like a kid caught sneaking candy, but the woman before her was a friend wearing a mischievous grin. Not a grandmother mad at her for missing curfew.

"I, uh…" She laughed. "I went on a date with Nate."

Sue Ellen put a hand on her hip, eyebrows rising to

her hairline. "I thought you two didn't want to go to the movie. What happened?"

"We ran into each other on the bus." Come to think of it, why had Nate been on her bus? He stayed on base. Had he been visiting someone?

"And…?" Sue Ellen prodded.

"And we talked and walked on the beach and had dinner." She kept the kiss part to herself. Though, since the tingles still ran all the way to her toes, her face *had* to be giving her away.

Sue Ellen's grin confirmed all suspicions.

Maddie threw herself down on the low couch. Never mind what had happened with Nate, as life-altering as the night felt at the moment. She was curious about the drive-in. "Come sit. Tell me about your date."

Sue Ellen gracefully rounded the couch, sitting in one of the side chairs. "We had a wonderful time. He's such an interesting man."

Maddie straightened. "So you love him?" As soon as the words left her mouth Maddie regretted them. Stupid.

"You're such a romantic." Sue Ellen laughed. "It's a little early for that, don't you think?"

Not according to the stories she'd heard all her life. Maddie sat back on the couch and regarded her grandmother. What had happened? Had her presence messed up the fairy tale that should have been Nana and Pops's romance, or had the years turned their stories whimsical?

If they hadn't fallen in love during their dance or their first date, then Maddie no longer knew what to believe.

Because if Nana and Pops hadn't immediately fallen in love, then maybe her entire view of what the perfect romance should look like had been flawed. The truth remained that they had married after only a short time. A matter of weeks, actually. But did that really mean they had been madly in love from the first moment? Or had they felt the sparks, liked what they knew about one another, and decided they could do the work to make their bond last a lifetime?

The thought sent shockwaves through her. In the modern times of dating everyone, sleeping around, and living together to test things out, the "jump straight to lifelong commitment" method seemed crazy. Simply find someone you connected with, marry them, and then determine to make your relationship work for the rest of your life? Unheard of.

Yet somehow, the approach had worked for her grandparents. Were they a one-in-a-million case? And if so, why wasn't Maddie watching the impossible romance unfold before her eyes?

"Sue Ellen, can I ask you something?"

Nana looked contemplative, as though she'd been mulling over something as well. "Sure."

"How can you tell if you want to marry a man?"

Her eyes widened, and she gave a small smile but sobered when Maddie didn't return her playful gesture. "Why do you ask?"

In this instance, she could probably tell the truth. At least, mostly. "My grandparents married after only three dates. I keep thinking, how could they be so sure so fast? How, after so short of a time, were they certain they wanted to spend their lives together?"

"Why don't you ask them?"

Maddie laughed to herself. She kinda was. "I've always heard the stories, and I found them beautiful. Honestly, until just now I never thought to ask. I assumed their love was so powerful and complete that they knew immediately. Perfect love at first sight, love so tangible that they knew right away they'd be together forever and nothing could ever tear them apart."

Sue Ellen looked skeptical but said nothing.

"I've been waiting for the same thing to happen to me." Maddie laughed at herself, feeling a little stupid. Or at least naïve. "I guess I figured that was the only way to recognize you'd found the right man. But now, I'm not so sure."

Sue Ellen watched her a moment. "You don't think that's how it happens? Instant clarity?"

"Do you?"

Sue Ellen puckered her lips. "I think that if we are honest with ourselves, we as women know exactly what kind of man we're looking for."

"We do?"

"Sure." She sat forward. "Think about it. What type of man would you never marry?"

Any of the ones she'd met online dating. "First, I'd have to marry a man of God. So anyone who isn't serious with his faith is off the list." Too many of the guys had called themselves Christians but couldn't tell her the last time they'd gone to church.

Sue Ellen nodded.

Maddie dug deep, trying to get past all the superficial things that clouded the truth of what she wanted. Attraction was important, sure, but lots of different types of men were physically attractive. Hair, skin, or eye color, face shape—none of that really mattered.

"I guess I wouldn't want to marry a man I sensed I couldn't trust." That had been the problem with a lot of the men she'd been on dates with. They'd tried to make their online profiles look like something different than who they actually were. If they needed to hide themselves to find women, then they weren't seeking the right one.

Sue Ellen nodded along. "See? We women harbor distinct hopes. Things we look for—even if we aren't aware we're searching for certain traits. Maybe that's why your grandparents moved so quickly. They found someone who met their hearts' requirements."

"Huh. Now that I'm thinking about it, you're totally right." She pulled her legs up under her on the couch and tucked her skirt under her ankles. She counted off on her fingers. "He'd be Christian, sincere, honest, and treat me with kindness. He'd be the kind of man his friends respected. He'd be a gentleman, probably a bit old-fashioned. He'd make me feel protected—like I could tell him anything because he'd always look out for my best interest."

*Oh my heavens. I've just described Nate.*

Sue Ellen smiled. "See?"

Maddie could hardly move. Her pulse thrummed in her ears. She'd never nailed down what she really wanted before, but now that she'd examined her true desires, Nate seemed to fit them all. But how could she *know*? For certain? She'd only just met the man. He could be hiding anything.

Pushing the thought away to examine later, Maddie flipped the question. "What about you? What are you looking for?"

"Many of the same qualities as you, actually. But I would also want a man who could make me laugh. He'd be the kind of man who, when life got hard, could remind me of all the good things worth enjoying."

Made sense. Nana had been born during the Great Depression. And Pops had always found ways to bring a smile to her face. She remembered countless times he'd stopped on the side of the road just to pick a pretty flower for his bride.

"I'd want a man who would have no problem

committing to me for the rest of his life," Sue Ellen said. "He'd be the steady type. Solid. Dependable."

"Handsome wouldn't hurt," Maddie said with a laugh.

Sue Ellen laughed with her. "No, sure wouldn't."

"So then," Maddie said, growing serious again. "Is that it? If you met a man who seemed to fulfill those requirements, he'd be the one?"

"Maybe." Nana shrugged. "I figure if nothing else, he'd be worth taking seriously."

"Not exactly what I'd call romantic, though. Takes the whole "falling head over heels in love" part out of dating."

"I certainly wouldn't jump to marrying anyone who didn't first fit what I was looking for, no matter how many sparks he made me feel. If all he had to offer was butterflies in the stomach, that wouldn't last." Sue Ellen gave her a wry smile. "My mother said that love wasn't just some warm feeling. Sure, that zing happens at times. But love is a mutual respect. A desire to put the other person's well-being first. If a man fit everything I knew I wanted, I wouldn't rely only on sweet feelings. Though I'd like those, too."

Again, the woman made sense.

Sue Ellen tapped her finger on her chin. "Yes, I do believe I'd consider very seriously a man who could show me he was capable of making my heart somersault but was also the type of man I could depend on even when those feelings mellowed."

Good to know. Must be why she'd accepted Pops's proposal. He'd given her a hint of the somersaults while also proving his merit. She'd certainly dampened Maddie's romantic view of the whole thing, but she made sense.

What an interesting way to look at finding a life partner. Did all the people of this era think that way? Couples in Nana's generation did seem to get married younger and stay together longer. Her own generation delayed marriage until thirty or beyond, and half of those still ended in divorce.

Had Nana just given her the secret to lasting love? The understanding that feelings would come and go and you had to build a life on mutual friendship and devotion first? Maybe. But that didn't guarantee the other person wouldn't run when their feelings changed.

Like her mother.

"Even if you met a man who seemed like he fulfilled all those ideals, how would you *really* know?" Maddie asked, leaning forward intently. How exactly had Nana been sure Pops would never hurt her? "What if he only seems that way but then later proves different? What if he commits but then one day decides he'd rather do something else?"

Sue Ellen thought a moment. "That's always possible."

How comforting.

"People grow. It takes years to deeply understand a person, and even then, that person changes. Just like we all do."

Great. So even if she found a good guy, he could turn into a dud at any moment. She crossed her arms.

Sue Ellen laughed. "But what do I know? I've never been married."

"You seem pretty wise to me." Even nearer her own age, Nana was more astute than Maddie had ever been. "That's scary though, right? If you marry a man too fast, then you're stuck with who he turns out to be."

"That's true of anything. Life is messy. Sometimes you take a chance and things don't turn out like you hope. Maybe things end badly." Sue Ellen gazed at her compassionately, and Maddie's heart twisted. "But I believe God has a purpose in all things. Even when people sin or make a mess of their relationships. There's still good to be found. Even if the only good is learning you are stronger than you ever thought possible because God Himself is your strength."

Wow. She'd never thought of it like that.

"I'd rather take the chance, work hard, and pray for the best. Do everything in my power to love the other person with everything I have. Then, in the end, if that wasn't enough, if he chose to leave or abandon me, then I could still have peace knowing I'd done everything I could. I'll honor God, and if everything fails, then He will still be there to pick up the pieces."

Maddie stared at her grandmother. Maybe that had been the key all along. Nana and Pops took a chance. They worked hard. They put God first. They'd been blessed. But what about her parents? Dad had honored God. Loved Mom even when she left. Tried to reconcile. Forgave her time and again. Finally, he'd been left with no choice but divorce.

Would he have changed anything? Would he have never married Mom at all? She wouldn't be here if he hadn't. And her father had shown her a real, rich faith through everything her mother had forced them to endure. Would Maddie be as solid in her own faith if not for his example?

"Something tells me you have a lot to think about." Sue Ellen patted her curls, looking as though she had a few things to consider herself.

Maddie smiled. "Captain Hall has me thinking about all kinds of things."

"Tell me about it." Sue Ellen wrapped her arms around her middle. "Major MacBride isn't like any other man I've met."

"Would you marry him, if he asked you?"

Sue Ellen laughed as if Maddie had said something completely ridiculous. But the woman would be proposed to in a matter of days, and she would say yes.

At least, that's how Maddie had always heard the story. Now, she wasn't so sure.

"You know what?" Sue Ellen slapped her hands

down on her thighs, and Maddie jumped. "I might. Not that I think he'd ever do something so spontaneous, but if Major MacBride pledged he'd commit to a lifetime of loving me, well…" She gave a timid smile in direct contradiction to her previous outburst. "I'd be inclined to believe he's the type of man who'd do his very best to keep such a promise."

And right there, Maddie had her answer. Nana had believed Pops to be a man of his word. If he said he'd do something, she believed he would. When Pops proposed, he'd tell Nana he would love her every day of his life. And she would take that risk and trust him. So far, he'd kept his promise.

If Maddie ever got home, she had a few more questions for Nana. Had Pops ever broken his pledge? Had they worked through hard times? Troubles? Betrayals? Maddie had always been so focused on the romance of their meeting that she'd never considered what all went into the relationship after the wedding.

"What about you? If Captain Hall asked you to be his bride, would you?"

If Nate promised he'd care for her every day of his life, if he made a vow to do his best to love her through good times and bad… She grinned at Nana. "You know what? I just might."

Nathanial stared at the ceiling, his mind refusing to settle and allow him to sleep. He'd prayed for wisdom and guidance. He'd asked God that if this strange, overwhelming feeling for Maddie wasn't in His will, then He'd scrub these desires from his brain and restore his senses.

He still couldn't get the woman out of his head. And not just the way she'd felt in his arms or the way he'd lost himself in her kiss. He thought about the way her eyes had sparkled as they'd talked over dinner until the restaurant closed.

They'd talked about their families and their pasts, their plans for the future. As though they'd been friends for years, he found he could talk to Maddie about anything. Conversation with her came with an ease he'd never before experienced. Talking to her felt like talking to his best friend. He'd been completely relaxed. Totally himself without trying to impress her.

The freedom of being in her company left him feeling nearly intoxicated.

They'd taken the last bus back to the base, and he'd walked her to her apartment just outside the gates. He'd wanted to kiss her again. Had seen the desire returned in her eyes. But he hadn't dared. Not when he already felt himself standing on a ledge with no parachute. Kissing her again tonight might have sent him off the edge, and he had a lot of thinking to do before he was ready to take a plunge like that.

What was she doing now?

Thinking of him? Did she feel the same as he did?

He shook his head. He better get hold of himself before he did anything crazy.

Like stay in the past to be with a woman he'd just met.

# Fourteen

Six days felt like a lifetime. How had she only been in 1956 for less than a week? In those few days, she'd sung in front of a crowd of people, been serenaded by a handsome man in uniform, had the kiss of her life, and gotten to know her grandmother in an entirely new way.

Every evening she went on walks with Nate. No more official dates, but when he'd finished his class for the day, he'd come by her apartment and they would walk around the base. She felt as though she'd known the man years, not days.

Talk about crazy.

Six days was also long enough for her to realize she could no longer put off decisions she needed to make. Living in the moment was nice, but she had to start making plans.

She watched Sue Ellen stir her coffee at their small kitchen counter. Her job as a waitress had kept her busy every night this week. But today she worked an earlier shift. And today Nana and Pops would have another date.

"Going out with the major tonight?" she asked.

Sue Ellen looked up from her coffee. "How did you know?"

Maddie laughed. "You have the night off. It doesn't take genius to put two and two together."

"I guess you're right." She dropped the spoon in the sink. "What about you?"

They hadn't discussed anything, but since Nate had been on the sidewalk below her door every night this week, she expected him at five fifteen looking dashing in his uniform. "I don't know."

"Why don't we four go out together? It would be fun."

Maddie grinned. "Sounds good." She checked her watch. "What time?"

"Robert is coming to pick me up at seven. But I'll give him a ring before I head to work and see what his plans are. I'd love for you two to come with us, and I'm sure he won't mind."

"I'll be back this afternoon. Just let me know the plan."

"I will." Sue Ellen blew on the top of her coffee. "Where are you going today?"

Sue Ellen had offered to get Maddie a job at the officers' club. Her boss was looking for another girl to help. Maddie had put her off since she'd expected to be back in the future by now. But each day that passed, she feared that might never be the case. And if so, she had to find a way to get word home to her family.

She had a feeling the only way to accomplish time-warp communications would be through the mysterious Victorian house that had sent her to the past. Especially since Mrs. Easley had never called. Maybe she'd written down the wrong number by accident.

"I have to take care of something this morning." She smoothed her hands down her light blue skirt. "But this afternoon, I'd like to come by the club and ask about that job. If you think that's all right."

Sue Ellen brightened. "That would be great. Mrs. Howard hasn't hired anyone else yet."

Remembering the stoic woman she'd auditioned for before the dance, she inwardly cringed. She looked like she'd be a harsh woman to work under. But she also seemed fair, even a little generous.

The payment Mrs. Howard had sent Maddie for performing at the dance had been much more than she'd expected, especially since things were so cheap in this time. Her first paying gig. She'd offered some of the funds to Nate, but he'd adamantly refused. Said he'd only been helping her out.

Regardless, if she was going to live here permanent-ly, she'd need a job. And she needed to tell her friends and grandparents. Somehow.

"I'll meet you there." Maddie grabbed her handbag

and stepped out in the hall, her mind swirling with crazy things she never thought she'd have to worry about.

How did one send a note to the future? If she stayed here, would she be one of Nana's friends who could then collaborate her own story? What did that mean for her parents? She would either completely screw up the future as she knew it or would end up meeting herself when she was born.

But she couldn't help any of that. She had no control over *when* she lived. Reminding herself she could only take one day at a time and do her best with the moments God had given her, Maddie made her way down the stairs and out into a warm September day.

She hummed as she strolled and then had a nice conversation with an elderly lady on the bus. By the time she reached The Depot, the sun peeked through the tops of the trees. She strolled up to the front porch and knocked on the door.

After once again receiving no answer, she rounded the back of the house and found the back door unlocked.

"Hello?" She called inside.

No one answered. Weird. Why leave the house open when no one was around? That didn't seem safe. Maybe people felt differently in the fifties. Or maybe Mrs. Easley left the house open for guests.

She stepped into the kitchen. Her own note to Mrs. Easley still sat on the kitchen counter, exactly where she'd left it. Goosebumps rose on her forearms. No one had been here since the last time she'd come by five days ago. Had Mrs. Easley been thrown into the past as well?

Maddie sank on a stool and stared at her note. What if the place had been full and the entire inn had been zapped to different times? She hadn't even considered that. Even the owner was missing. At least, in this time.

Were there a bunch of people here in the house, just in different years?

She placed her head in her hands. "I could use a little help, God. I've been trying to enjoy what I have here, but I'm a little scared. What do I do?"

She waited a few moments, but no great revelations came. Forcing herself to focus, Maddie tried to figure out how to do what she'd come for. An idea struck. Of course. She would pull a Marty McFly. In the movie, that professor guy had mailed a package from the Wild West to be delivered to Marty in the future. The post office had held the package all those years and delivered the envelope on time.

Would the same thing work for her? Probably not. In real life, they'd either deliver the letter immediately or throw it away as undeliverable.

For good measure, she returned to her room and looked in the mirror again, but nothing happened. Curious about any other people staying here, she knocked on the room next to hers. No one answered.

She tried the knob. Unlocked. She poked her head inside. "Hello? Anyone here?"

Silence. She looked around. Furnished similarly to hers, this room held a queen bed, a dresser, a wardrobe, and a writing desk. And a mirror on the wall. A perfect twin to the one in her room—on what looked to be the same spot on the wall on this side.

Interesting. She studied her reflection. Tried a little wave. The reflection did the same. So much for the wild idea that maybe the mirror on this side of the wall was the return end of the time tunnel.

She touched the frame anyway and wasn't surprised to feel the cool glass. She turned to leave, but an open book on the desk caught her attention. Some kind of textbook. Something about planes and military history. She held her finger in the page and looked at the cover.

AIR FORCE WEATHER
OUR HERITAGE 1937 TO 2012

Maddie's mouth went dry. A training manual. And *not* from 1956.

MEETING THE CHALLENGE FOR 75 YEARS

She flipped open a few pages and scanned the table of contents, her eyes lingering on "Chapter 3, Chronology 1947–1956."

She stared at the book. Only relatively a few years old. Or here, too many years new. She glanced around the room. Had whoever occupied this room also disappeared into the past? Had to, given the date on this book. They didn't seem to be here in the fifties. From the date on the manual, they were probably from 2012.

Had that person gone back sixty-five years as well? She did the math. Whoever'd been here would be in 1947.

Unless of course they'd been reading an older version of the book. Regardless, where had they gone? No one occupied the inn.

But then, she hadn't stayed here either. Whoever rented this room could have woken up somewhere nearby. Just as she had. Someone who'd owned an Air Force training manual.

Could Nate…? She immediately dismissed the thought. He was clearly a man of the fifties. Too gentlemanly to be a millennial. Too classy and mature to be like any of the guys of her generation. If anyone she'd met had been from the future, it was *not* Nathanial Hall.

But still…this was a military book. Air Force. Nate was Air Force.

*So are half the men in this town.*

She closed the book and thought a moment. If this book was here in this time, did it also exist in the future? Worth a shot. She sat at the desk and found a pad of paper and a pen inside.

*Dear person who owns this book,*

*I'm sure this is going to sound very weird, but I am stuck in the past, in 1956 to be exact. If you've experienced anything in this old house like I have, maybe you won't find my statement so bizarre after all. I'd like to ask you a favor, should you find yourself back in the present.*

She frowned. What if this book went to 2012? Too early to catch herself here. She shrugged. Close enough. Give or take a decade.

*Will you deliver a message to my grandparents, please? They live just down this road. House number 607, Robert and Sue Ellen MacBride. Please let them know I'm alive, and I will come home. If I can.*

Maddie stared at the words. Crazy. If anyone found this, they'd think she had lost her mind. But maybe they'd be curious enough to walk down a few houses to find out.

She signed her name and set the note squarely on the cover of the book. Maybe whoever had this room would figure out how to get home from wherever they'd gone. Maybe someone else would find it some other year. What if the letter had already magically appeared in the future because the book existed outside of time?

In this place, who could tell?

All she could do was pray her family didn't suffer

while she figured out what to do about her situation.

Back downstairs, she pulled the door closed behind her and exited around the back of the house. She drew a long breath and made her decision. Time to get to the officers' club.

She'd be starting a new life.

Nathanial paced the sidewalk outside Maddie's building. Five thirty. Where was she? They'd met down here at five fifteen every day this week. Had she forgotten?

"Nate!"

At the sound of Maddie's voice, he turned. She and Sue Ellen bustled down the sidewalk, their cheeks flushed. She reached for his hand as she approached, and he gripped her fingers. The sight of her immediately brought a smile.

"You all right?"

She puffed out a breath that stirred small strands of hair around her face. "Yes. Sorry. Mrs. Howard hired me on the spot and insisted I get to work right away. We got here as soon as our shift was over and the woman finished going over a list of rules." She flashed him an apologetic smile. "Thanks for waiting."

He opened his mouth, but Sue Ellen spoke first. "Would you be terribly put out if we asked you to wait a little longer, Captain?"

"Oh, yes," Maddie said before he could answer. "Sue Ellen and Robert asked us to go on a double date tonight." Uncertainty flashed in her eyes. Probably because of the way he'd rejected that same offer the first time.

"That sounds great," he said quickly. "I'll run back to my room and change into civilian clothes. What time should I pick you up?"

Relief, followed by joy, washed over Maddie's face. That was one of the things he loved about her. She never tried to hide her emotions. She wore how she felt in every sparkle of her eyes, every expression that caressed her face. Maddie never made him guess what she was thinking.

"Robert will be here at seven."

He gave Maddie's fingers a squeeze. "I'll meet you then."

The girls hurried inside their building, and he jogged back to his lodging. He was dressed with plenty of time to spare, so he walked down to the BX and paid a dime for a newspaper, then settled on a bench outside to read.

*Thursday, September 20, 1956*

He scanned the headlines, skipped over some entertainment news about Elvis, and turned to the weather page.

*Tropical depression moves into the mouth of the Gulf. Meteorologists suspect the storm will gain strength and make landfall in the coming days.*

Saturday, the Hurricane Hunters would fly into the storm to collect data. He had to get on that flight manifest. He tapped the newspaper on his knee. If he went up with them, maybe he'd have a chance to save them.

Or he'd go down with the rest of the crew.

What would Maddie do if he'd come to the past only to die? Did he believe strongly enough that he could change the past to risk his future?

But honestly, that risk would be true of any mission he flew. Any storm they encountered. Any flight could be his last. He couldn't live in fear of dying or he'd be useless.

He stared at the paper a little longer, not really reading.

When it was time to meet the girls, he left the paper on the bench for the next fellow and walked back through the base and out the front gate, nodding to the airman on duty as he passed. Maddie lived off base, just two blocks before the White House Hotel.

He found Mac pacing the same section of sidewalk outside the door. "Hello, sir."

Mac turned. "How's it going, Nate?"

Had they all started calling him by Maddie's nickname? Not that he minded. People had always called him by his given name, but surprisingly he found he rather liked the friendliness of the shortened version.

He thrust out his hand. "We have a date with some pretty girls. I'd say I'm doing all right."

Mac laughed as he shook Nathanial's hand. "Ain't that the truth."

"I saw in the paper we've got a storm building in the Gulf. Your crew flying out to take readings?"

"Should be pretty soon." His eyebrows dipped in thought. "Why?"

Might as well be honest. Or as honest as he could be without sounding crazy. "I'd like to go. My goal is to become a Hurricane Hunter myself, and I figured some flight time would be good for me."

Mac stroked his chin. "I'll see what I can do."

Blood zipped through his veins. One step closer. He couldn't help the feeling that he was meant to fly with them into that storm. But he'd need a little help.

*God, if this is your plan, help me get on that plane. And come back alive.*

# Fifteen

$\mathcal{M}$addie could get used to life here. This time of classy clothing and gentlemen who pulled out chairs. Maddie sat on a cushioned seat at a cute little seaside restaurant and gave Nate a smile. Oh, how her heart fluttered for this man.

Nana's words kept circling in her head. Nate exhibited all the characteristics she wanted. He was honest, trustworthy, made her smile, and sent her senses tripping all over themselves. What more could a girl want?

"This is a nice place, Robert," Sue Ellen said as she settled down next to Maddie.

"Nice place for a nice girl." He winked.

Maddie withheld her laugh. Who knew Pops had been so cheesy? They were adorable, smiling at one another with moon eyes. She glanced at Nate, who perused his menu, ignoring the romantic way the other couple interacted.

She turned her eyes on her own menu. Her eyebrows rose at the prices at Gus Stevens. She could get a steak dinner, half a stuffed lobster, and three or four appetizers for less than the cost of a number one at Chick-fil-A.

"Decide what you want?" Nate asked.

"Not yet. How about you?" Better to see what price he paid for a meal and go from there.

"Think I'll get the dozen fried oysters with french fried potatoes."

She found his selection in the seafood portion of the menu. One dollar. Wow. How much had she tipped that bus driver when she'd dropped a dollar in his bucket? She really needed to get a handle on the value of things if she was going to live here.

The thought brought a surprising pang of home-sickness. How could she possibly miss home when the two people she loved most in the world sat across the table from her?

The restaurant was filled with patrons, the atmos-phere lively. People laughed while waiters scooted around the tables. Maddie had everything she could want in this moment, yet something deep inside troubled her. A longing to be where she belonged with the grandparents she knew.

What if she could take Nate back to the future with her? That would be perfect. Her spark of hope fizzled. She didn't even know how to get herself home, much less bring back a life-sized—and very much alive—

souvenir.

No, better she keep the truth to herself. Forever. If anyone ever found out where she'd really come from, who she really was, the knowledge could ruin everything. Then what would she do? She couldn't be stuck in the past alone.

"Big menu, right?" Nate asked with a chuckle.

What? Oh, yeah. He wanted to know her choice. She forced herself to focus and picked the first thing priced the same as the meal he'd chosen. "Fried shrimp for me."

"Good choice." He winked at her.

Maddie drew in a long breath of air laced with the tangy scents of seafood. A new life. Friends. And a man who could be her match. Staying here would be a blessing.

Setting the menu aside, she smiled at her grandparents. They were talking about an upcoming storm.

Jumping into the conversation, she asked, "What storm?"

"There's a system moving into the Gulf," Pops said. "Should hit early next week."

She nodded. Storms hit the coast all the time. Probably not a big deal, or they would have heard more about it.

The waiter came to take their drink orders and then scurried off.

"Will you be flying in?" Sue Ellen asked, picking up

the conversation again.

Pops nodded. "Probably on Saturday."

Maddie frowned. "Flying in? What are you talking about?"

"Hurricane Hunters," Nate supplied. "They'll go in and take a reading."

Maddie sat back in her seat. What? No. No that didn't make sense at all. Pops wasn't a Hurricane Hunter. He was a pilot. Like, a regular pilot. Right?

She thought back but couldn't remember Nana or Pops ever talking about him flying into hurricanes. She shook her head. "I'm sorry, I must have misunderstood. Are you saying that you are going to fly a plane *into a hurricane*?"

Pops chuckled. "That's what we do. The readings will help people prepare."

Maddie gaped at him. How had she never known this? Flying into a storm was crazy. He could get himself killed! As soon as the thought erupted, she had to stifle a chuckle at her own silliness. Pops was alive and well in the future. Whatever this crazy storm-flying thing was, he would be fine. Obviously.

Unless something had changed and the past had shifted. Was that possible? She thought her presence could only produce another version of the future. Not create different versions of the past.

"How long have you been a Hurricane Hunter?" she asked carefully.

"Since fifty-three." He nodded toward Nate. "Might be taking this instructor up with us, if I can get him approved."

Nate had mentioned something about training to be a Hurricane Hunter the night he'd told her about his father. She hadn't paid much attention to that part.

She studied her grandfather. Pops had been doing this for years. So she hadn't made any changes. For some reason, her grandparents had never mentioned this part of Pops's job history. She would have remembered something like this.

Why hadn't they said anything? The possibly unpleasant reasons made her nervous, though she couldn't exactly explain why.

Sue Ellen didn't seem at all concerned with the prospect of Pops purposely flying into a hurricane. She sat with her hands folded, her face peaceful. How could she be so calm? Maddie knew Pops would be fine, but right now Nana couldn't have any clue.

The other part of Pops's statement hit her in the chest.

"Wait." She stared at Nate. "You want to go on this death mission, too?"

He frowned, and she immediately regretted the words. It would be fine. Had to be. She knew the future. So why did the idea of Nate going along make her stomach flop?

Nate's eyebrows tightened, and the strong lines of

his face hardened. "I intend to become a Hurricane Hunter myself." He looked at her as though her forgetting his goal had offended him.

"What we do saves lives," Pops interjected. "Besides, we're military men. Danger is part of the job."

Sure. He'd been in occupied Japan after the war. Had done tours all over the world. Danger was nothing to Pops. He'd go for months to Vietnam and…

She stared at Nate, bile rising in her throat. Oh no. Why hadn't she thought about any of that? Here she was preparing for a future with this man, in this time. But she'd forgotten about all the things that would come. The long periods of time Nana had spent alone while Pops completed tour after tour.

Did she want that life? Could she see herself with a man who would leave her at a moment's notice? Who would always put his duty above even his own life?

Above her?

The waiter came and took their orders, but Maddie hardly noticed. Pops ordered for Nana and Nate did the same for her. She probably would have found that charming, if not for the way her insides felt like mush.

For all that she'd found perfect about this man, she'd overlooked one glaring truth. He was a military man. Would go to war. Might never come back. Would he end up in a Vietnam POW camp? Forever lost?

Even though he wouldn't know the outcomes of the coming wars as she did, he would still choose to leave her again and again whenever duty called. He would always pick his job over her.

Nana and Pops had survived that life. But could she? Would she be willing to pack up and move wherever the Air Force sent him? Would she be willing to wait for him at base after base, with no family and no friends to support her while he deliberately put himself in danger?

The food was good, and the people at her table had fun, but the night had been dampened for Maddie. She tried to share in their love of the moment, but the nagging inside her wouldn't go away.

She could never love a military man, because he would always break her heart.

# Sixteen

After supper, Pops suggested another walk on the beach. Maddie put her hand in Nate's arm, her heart twisting the entire time.

"Are you all right?" he whispered in her ear.

She nodded. Okay, that was a lie. "I can't stop thinking about this Hurricane Hunter thing. It sounds dangerous."

They made their way across the road and to the coastline. This was a different stretch of beach than they'd visited before, but once she crossed onto the sand, none of that mattered. There was something constant about the ocean. Calming. And she needed to settle her nerves. The salty air caressed her face, drawing some of the heat from her cheeks.

"Firefighting is dangerous," Nate said slowly. "So is police work. Yet those jobs are important."

The conviction in his voice reminded her what he'd said about his father. The police officer. Did he seek danger and an early death as some kind of tribute to the dad he'd lost?

Frustration swelled inside her. "Well, yes, but we have radar systems. Flying into a hurricane seems unnecessary."

He remained silent. She didn't mean to disregard his dreams, but didn't he see how ridiculous flying a plane into hundred-mile-per-hour winds was?

"Do you know the difference between a storm that kills hundreds and one that only damages property?" His voice, calm and even, seemed filled with steel.

She watched Nana and Pops walk in front of them, laughing. Did Nana ever worry about these things? Was that why Pops had never mentioned this crazy hurricane thing? Nana had shown him what a senseless risk he was taking and he'd quit?

But Pops still went on different missions. Fought wars.

She removed her hand from Nate's arm and stared out over the glistening waves, sparkling with the final rays of the day's sun. "I suppose you're going to tell me the difference is a few men who fly a plane into the storm."

The words were snippy, she knew. And totally unfair. But she couldn't help it. Of course this would be how things turned out. As soon as everything seemed perfect, something would come along and burst her bubble. How stupid she'd been. Too blinded by slippery feelings to see the truth about the core nature of the man at her side. The man who sang Sinatra and opened doors for her was also a man who wouldn't hesitate to abandon her.

Probably better she face the realities now before she got any further entangled with this man. Her heart wrenched, refusing to accept the truth. She ground her teeth.

"Not entirely." He took a few steps down the sand, and after a moment she walked beside him again. "But the more information we have, the more we can prevent needless loss of life."

What about the needless loss of *his* life? "I don't understand. Aren't you an instructor? Why would you need to go out on this trip?"

The muscle in his jaw convulsed, and she could see she'd hit a nerve. But she needed to understand what drove him to do such things. Because the kind of man who would choose to put himself in this kind of danger would always make the same choice.

"It's important. I think I can help."

Savior complex. She should have known. She stared at Nana and Pops ahead of them. The thought of losing Nate felt like lead in her stomach. Would she let the risk of losing him in his duty make her turn away from him now? Would she forsake what they could have for fear of her broken heart later?

Nana and Pops had made a military life work. Many couples did. Why couldn't she?

Question was, would she want to?

*Should have thought of that before you let yourself care about an Air Force man.*

She shook her head. Why was she even worrying about this decision today? They weren't the ones who would marry after a few dates. Why in the world was she getting herself all worked up for nothing?

"I'm sorry." She forcefully pushed aside feelings that would do her no good. "Your job is none of my business."

Today. She would focus on today. This moment. Nothing more.

His brow creased.

Maddie forged ahead, trying to convince herself with each word. "You're very brave and selfless to choose a career that puts others before yourself. I'm sure your father would be proud." She flashed him a smile and hurried to catch up to her grandparents.

After a moment, Nate jogged up beside her. "You are a confusing woman."

Said the man who wanted to fly a plane into a hurricane. "Sorry. I realized I was speaking out of place and ruining the evening. Sometimes I think too much." She reached for his hand. "Can we just start over and pretend I didn't make a fool of myself?"

She tried for a bright smile, but Nate didn't look like he was buying it. "This really bothers you." It was a statement not a question. "Why?"

No way could she tell him all the things she'd been thinking. She'd send him running for sure if she started spouting nonsense about worrying about what her life would be like married to him. But how did she answer the question truthfully?

"I guess the entire idea took me by surprise. I'd never heard of such a thing until you mentioned it the other day, and then I didn't actually realize what the job entailed until tonight." She shook her head again, though the action still hadn't cleared her brain. "But like I said, it wasn't my place to attack your profession or question your motives. I'm sorry."

Nate remained thoughtful and they walked hand in hand. What was she going to do? Keep falling for this man—because she was pretty sure that was what was happening to her and why she'd overreacted—or realize she couldn't live the only life he would be able to offer and stop this now?

"I think you're worried that something will happen. That someone will get hurt."

Well, duh. She nodded.

"But that's only because you care about people." He bumped her shoulder. "Am I right?"

Her mouth went dry. "I, uh… Yeah." Her cheeks burned but she pushed through. "Yeah. I do care about you. I know we just met, but I don't like the idea of something happening to you."

He smiled as if he'd just won some kind of victory.

"I care about you, too. And I promise I take every precaution and consider the dangers before a mission."

She sighed. "I understand." She glanced at her grandparents laughing ahead. "And I know it will be fine. I just…worry." The words stuck in her throat. She couldn't tell him she knew this mission would be fine because the pilot was still alive and well sixty-five years from now.

The true reason she'd been upset hadn't been this coming storm but the thought of the one after it. All the other storms he'd want to fly into.

Nate wrapped an arm around her shoulder. Then he started to whistle. She glanced up at him. He flashed her a smile and started to sing. His rich voice caressed the words of "The Way You Look Tonight" over her, and she felt as though the song had been written just for her.

He pulled her close, and her heart somersaulted.

The lyrics pushed into her heart, lifting her mood. He knew she worried about him. Cared about him. And rather than driving him away, here he was trying to lift her mood. She snuggled closer into him. This man. He would make her risk heartbreak just for the chance to savor moments like this.

Nana turned back and watched them, her face bright. Pops chuckled, but Nate didn't seem to care. He lifted his voice higher.

He spun her around in the sand, and Maddie laughed, forgetting everything the future might hold for them as she fell into the moment. Her feet glided in the sand, and her hair flew out behind her, tangling in the wind. He tucked her neatly back into his side.

"What's that song?" Pops called.

Nate's voice stopped. His eyes widened as though he'd been caught in something. But his expression changed back to a smile so quickly she thought she must have imagined his discomfort. He cleared his throat. "Just a little melody."

Weird. That was one of Sinatra's most famous songs. Didn't Nana and Pops know it? Before she could ask, Nate spun her around in another circle and dipped her back.

He leaned over her, his eyes dark pools that threatened to make her forget everything else. His words whispered over her face. "I don't know what it is about you, Miss Maddie Palmer, that makes me do such uncharacteristic things."

Would he kiss her? Her toes dug into the sand, and she stared at his lips, longing for them to find hers.

He placed her back upright and pulled her by the hand. Her heart fluttered. *Oh my.* She might very well endure anything for moments like this.

She pushed the disturbing thought away to examine later. For now, this moment was enough. Had this been how Nana felt? That the moments spent with Pops were enough, no matter what? She watched them up ahead. Had Nana had these same fears but decided Pops was worth the risk?

Nate chuckled. "Looks like you have high hopes for those two, the way you keep watching them."

Maddie laughed. He had no idea. "Sure do. They're going to have a wonderful life together." Oh boy. That came off as a little weird. "At least, I hope so." She laughed, the sound wobbly, even to her own ears.

Nate's eyes narrowed slightly, then all of a sudden he grinned again. What was with him tonight?

"*She's got high hopes*," he belted out, his rich voice rising on the breeze. "*High hopes*." Grinning, he nudged her shoulder.

Unable to help herself, Maddie picked up Nate's version of the silly song. "*She's got high apple pie in the sky hopes*."

Nate wiggled his eyebrows, and they sang the lines of the rubber tree plant song together.

Maddie laughed. Nate joined her, then stopped short, his face an odd mixture of confusion and shock.

"What?"

"You know that song."

Warning bells went off in her head. But she couldn't have sung anything out of time, because he'd known the song too. She took a step back, her heart hammering.

"But see, funny thing is…" Nate took a step closer, eyes roaming her face. "That song wasn't—" He stopped short. Tilted his head. "Where did you hear that song?"

The color drained from Maddie's already pale face, and her large eyes searched his. Things she'd said fell into place. The more she'd gone on about the storm, the more his mind started to pull up little oddities he'd kept ignoring. Songs she'd played at the dance. Little things she'd said that had seemed out of place.

Her fears about the flight into the storm. Did she know more than she would say? Did she know the flight was doomed? That the plane would go down, killing the entire crew?

Was that why she worried so much?

Questions fired through his head, peppering his senses with possibilities. Could she also be from the future? From his time?

"I, uh." Maddie shook her head. Her mouth twisted to the side.

He should have seen the signs sooner. The song she'd played on the piano the night of the dance had rattled around in the back of his brain for days. A song he couldn't place but knew. A song that wasn't from the fifties.

And then he remembered the time when she'd called Sinatra songs *classics*.

They stared at one another. How could he ask her the obvious without giving himself away? Because if he was wrong, she would think he was crazy.

He could lose her. The thought kept him from blurting out anything. Because with each passing moment, he wondered more and more if he even wanted to try to get back to the future. Because Maddie Palmer was in the past.

"I don't remember," she finally said, though the words seemed to pain her. She narrowed her eyes. "Where did *you* hear that song?"

She was trying to trap him. Was he certain the rubber tree song had been recorded in 1959 for *A Hole in the Head*? He hadn't seen the movie in years. Could it have been earlier? Did he remember the release date wrong?

"I saw it in a movie."

She blinked at him. "Which one?"

Was she playing games? "*A Hole in the Head.* Sinatra sings it."

Maddie laughed nervously. "Oh. I don't remember the movie. Maybe I heard it somewhere else."

He was pretty sure that movie hadn't come out yet. But not sure enough to expose himself. He took another angle. "What was that song you played on the piano at the dance?"

"Which one?"

If he knew the name, he wouldn't have asked. "One you didn't sing to."

Something flashed in her eyes. Worry? "Sorry. I

played several of those. One from Judy Garland?"

"No."

She swallowed and turned her head on a swivel. "We lost the others. We better catch up."

Maddie darted away before he could stop her. He hurried after her, his feet sliding in the sand. The woman moved like a gazelle. Did that make him the lion?

"Maddie! Please." He reached for her, and his fingers brushed the silky mass of her hair.

She stopped and held his gaze. Something sparked between them. Something weird and irrational. Completely illogical and yet compellingly magnetic. He couldn't deny the feelings that tethered him to her. Or the undeniable notion that, if he didn't fix this now, the loss of her would rip him to shreds.

The idea made no sense. None. He hardly knew her. But even though he didn't belong in this time—and maybe she didn't either—he couldn't risk losing whatever was happening between them.

He reached for her hand, and she let him hold her fingers between his palms. He searched her eyes. "What's going on?"

She laughed, but even he could tell she was faking the humor. "I don't know what you mean." She blinked at him, momentarily hiding pools of blue confusion. "Look, I'm sorry I don't remember all the songs I played the other night. Some were ones I learned a long time ago from my piano teacher. Some were her own songs."

He nodded, though he couldn't say for sure if he believed her or merely wanted to.

"And as for the rubber tree song, I remember now." She brightened. "It came from a musical I saw on Broadway." She licked her lips.

Was she lying? Maybe the song had been on Broadway before the movie. He couldn't remember. It wasn't as if he'd studied up on the fifties before coming here.

Maddie's eyes drew him in. Casting a spell on his senses and sending him into a tailspin.

What was more likely? He'd gotten the dates mixed up and freaked Maddie out, or Maddie had also made an impossible time jump?

One scenario seemed far more likely than the other. He shook his head. "Sorry. You're right."

He started walking again and tried to convince himself he was imagining things. But… he cast a sidelong glance at her. Something was off. He felt it in his gut.

But what was he supposed to do? Accuse her of being a time traveler?

# Seventeen

*H*ad Nathanial ruined everything with Maddie? Their date hadn't been what he'd hoped. Nothing like what he'd pictured. She'd gotten upset with him, then avoided him the rest of the night after the awkward conversation about the rubber tree song. Their parting at her door had been stiff. Cold. Thoughts had churned behind her eyes, but whatever they were, she hadn't shared them. And he hadn't asked.

He finished lacing his boots and tucked his hat under the arm of his olive drab flight suit. Early morning air still crisp with dew awakened his senses. He breathed through the familiar pre-mission adrenaline pumping in his veins as he walked through the base toward the flight line. But not only the anticipation of the flight had his pulse spiking.

The more he thought about their date, the more he berated himself for not speaking his mind. If she thought him an idiot, so what? Better he be open and real than play games. If they were going to have any kind of future together, she'd have to know the truth of where—or rather, when—he'd come from.

If he was going to plunge into the crazy feelings rolling through him like the storm building over the Gulf, then he could accept no less than complete honesty from them both.

As soon as he got back from this mission, Maddie Palmer wouldn't get to avoid him any longer.

She'd worked every night since their date. He'd tried calling. Had gone by the officers' club. Her smile had been warm, but her attention limited. Why hadn't he stayed around after her shift? Walked her home?

Truth be told, he'd been a coward. Thrown himself into his work like he did every time life got messy. Work offered order, predictability, and structure.

His feelings for Maddie fit in none of those categories, and he wasn't sure how to handle them. So instead of dealing with them, he'd put his energy into completing his classes for the day and preparing for this morning's flight. Giving his head and heart time to work through these unusual stirrings.

Telling himself he still had time.

But he'd waited too long. His last words to her hadn't been to tell her how he felt or the truth about his circumstances. He'd merely let her walk away.

Now he might never see her again.

Casting those thoughts aside for later, he pushed the door open to the flight line shack and made his way to the large chalkboard that would designate today's flights.

He scanned the board for the Magnolia Mayhem's tail number and confirmed the block time.

"You going up today, Captain?"

Nathanial turned to find a master chief obviously a member of the MOC—maintenance operation center—holding a clipboard.

"Sure am. Captain Nathanial Hall. Riding along with the Mayhem."

The dark-haired man checked the manifest for his name and then gave a nod. "All set. Have a good flight, sir."

Nathanial thanked him and pushed down the large lock-release bar to open the security door leading out to the flight line.

If he made it back alive, he'd tell her everything. If he didn't, well, God had a plan in all things.

Three birds sat on the tarmac, their metal wings shining in the first whispers of dawn. One would rotate with the Magnolia Mayhem for recon duty, and the other would likely be evacuated later today before the storm moved in.

He gave his name to a wizened crew chief and received a curt nod to continue on his way. Wind ruffled the white wisps of the man's hair as he shouted to the flight engineer about any diagonals or red crosses—items that would need to be addressed prior to takeoff.

The men continued the preflight check, leaving

Nathanial to wait on the crew to arrive. Mac had gotten him a ride on this trip—letting him gain some flight time for his application and a real look at what the Hurricane Hunters did before he signed up to fly on a crew of his own.

Worry skittered over his nerves. He had no idea what to expect. No clue what had gone wrong in flight that had caused the Magnolia Mayhem to go down. Would he be able to alter the outcome?

Or was he walking into a suicide mission?

He couldn't think about that now. He had a chance to save the lives of five other men, and he intended to make the best of the opportunity.

The WB-29 Superfortress sat on the tarmac as the flight engineer and the crew chief talked about their lists and when they expected to pull chocks. The four-engine giant had been a bomber during the war but had been reconfigured as a reconnaissance plane. Nathanial had encountered a few of these old girls at museums but had never thought he'd go up in the air in one. Into a hurricane.

The prospect of seeing the inside of a cyclone had his fingers twitching.

A van pulled up and came to a stop, and the flight crew bustled out. These five men had completed their briefing at base ops and would be ready to take to the sky as soon as the crew chief gave the go-ahead.

Mac approached and slapped him on the shoulder.

"Ready to log in some flight time?"

He chuckled. "Yes, sir. Appreciate the chance to go up with you today."

Mac grinned. "Run should take us about six hours." He gave him a wink. "We'll get the girls when we get back and take them out for a nice dinner."

So he hoped. "Sounds good, sir." He gave a nod to the aircraft. "Mind if I have a look at the equipment before we go up?"

With the proper permissions, he climbed the ladder and entered the massive plane. This old girl would be the last of her kind. Even if she wasn't destined to go down today, the B-29s wouldn't be used much longer. Not past this year, if he remembered correctly. Soon, the tired B-29s would be replaced by a modification of B-50Ds and WB-50 configurations.

Inside, the interior of the Magnolia Mayhem had been retrofitted from a war machine to a weather recon unit. With the armament and related equipment removed, she had been re-designated as a WB-29. Additional radio and specialized meteorological equipment had been installed.

This tiny portion of the plane with the blocky equipment would be his staging ground for one unconventional rescue mission. Which he had no idea how he planned to execute. Diving blind into an op wasn't his speed. He was a man of planning and forethought. But he had to try.

He carefully examined the equipment, just in case anyone had missed any deficiencies he might be able to spot. At least they had the Very High Frequency (VHF) pilot-to-forecaster service installed. That would make communication with Mac and his copilot faster and more reliable. He took a seat where the ARWO—Aerial Reconnaissance Weather Officer—would gather data. Too bad he didn't have access to some 3D modulations and advanced radar.

They would be using an AN/APN-82 Doppler radar and AN/AMQ-7 airborne temperature-humidity indicators. A far cry from the kind of equipment he was used to. But with a modern meteorology degree, maybe his knowledge would come in handy.

Still, he was glad he'd been studying up on his history and knew something about the operation of this equipment. The radar wouldn't be as sophisticated as what he was used to back home, but having spent over a week training men in the use of the equipment installed in the Magnolia Mayhem, he felt confident he could operate the systems if need be. Maybe something had happened to the weather officer during the flight.

The flight crew entered the plane to take their positions. A young man Nathanial guessed to be in his early to mid-twenties approached with Mac.

"You'll be shadowing our newbie here," Mac said to Nathanial. "Lieutenant Preston got his sign-off last week and is ready for his first solo run with us." He slapped the man on the shoulder.

The wide-faced lieutenant gave a nod to Nathanial. "Glad to have you with us, Captain."

Nathanial strapped on his vintage headset and sent a prayer for safety heavenward as the rest of the crew settled into their positions. The superfortress's four massive engines whirred to life.

"Keesler Tower," a man's voice crackled over the com. "Winds 180 at 5, altimeter 29.95. You're cleared for takeoff, runway two one. Climb and maintain two thousand, runway heading."

The roar of the engines increased, and he braced himself for the lurch. Birds this big were heavy and would need most of the one-mile runway to get off the ground. When Mac let off on the brakes, they shot forward.

Nathanial settled in as the plane gained altitude and watched the young LT check his equipment. With the storm still at the mouth of the Gulf, it would take them an hour or so to reach any turbulence. And, according to his training manual, he had at least that much longer to live.

He spent the time praying for the crew's safety and thinking about Maddie.

As they hurdled toward the deadly storm, he thought about the storm his heart had been suffering. He'd prayed about Maddie for days, and God hadn't warned him away from the feelings swirling within him.

No, he'd been doing that all on his own. Avoiding the truth because he was afraid of the risk.

Yet here he was willing to risk his life for five strangers when he'd been too much of a coward to risk his heart with a woman who might—or might not—be from the right time.

But what was *the right time* anyway? God had sent him here. Maybe the fifties was his right time because Maddie was here. God alone could have brought the two of them together like this.

Hurtling himself toward an almost certain death brought sharp clarification. Life was short. Too short not to be radically honest—with himself and with her—and make the most of every moment. A weight slid off him as he came to a determination.

If he survived, he wouldn't risk losing another moment with her. He wanted Maddie Palmer at his side for every moment God granted. Too soon or not, as soon as they touched the ground back at Keesler, he'd ask that woman to marry him. And he'd stay here to build a life with her.

That settled, he turned his focus back to the matter at hand. If he was going to be a groom, he had to first get this plane home.

He watched the readings of the flight-level data from the aircraft's weather instruments. The LT seemed adept and kept a close eye on the changing systems. So far, Nathanial couldn't see anything that the man hadn't already made note of.

As they neared the storm, the weather officer kept a close watch on the radar, keeping them clear of any severe thunderstorm cells and dangerous turbulence. Would a random storm on the outer bands have caused the Mayhem to go down?

The skies began to darken, warning of the impending cyclone and the deadly storms whipping around the eye.

Nathanial mentally calculated an escape vector as they drew closer to Flossy. Mac came over the system, letting them know they were about to enter the storm. With one more prayer for guidance and protection, he braced himself for whatever would come next.

"When we get close to the eye," Mac said through his headset, "Lieutenant Preston will take us in. We're about to start our descent to 10,000 feet. Weather, your briefing?"

Nathanial studied the LT across from him. As the crew's Aerial Reconnaissance Weather Officer, it would be up to him to make sure this bird survived the storm.

The man's brows gathered, then he pressed a button to speak over the inflight line. "We're going to need to enter our first fix thirty nautical miles south of the expected position. Navigator, you'll need to adjust the flight plan accordingly."

The plane began its descent to 10,000 feet from the 24,000 foot cruise altitude and slowed to 180 knots.

Inbound toward the eye of the storm.

Through the small window, Nathanial watched the sea below churn. White caps, patches of foam, and the spitting spray evidenced the power of the furious winds.

"There's a particularly nasty thunderstorm ahead," Lieutenant Preston said. "Navigation, course correct."

"Negative. Current trajectory steers us clear."

Nathanial tensed. Had the navigator refused to listen to the weather officer? Had the man's arrogance gotten this crew killed?

"No need to tempt death," the LT said as he studied the radar again, seemingly unfazed by the other officer's comment.

Nathanial fought a growing sense of unease as he shifted his focus to the small window next to his seat. He might not be overly familiar with the vintage equipment, but the makeup of a hurricane hadn't changed in the past sixty-five years.

He knew weather formations and cloud shapes. Spiral bands of thunderstorms would wrap around a bright ring surrounding a clear spot—the eyewall, containing the most violent weather in the storm.

Heavy rain pelted the metal casing of the airplane, pounding like a giant demanding to be let inside. Sheets of water washed over his window, obscuring the wrathful seas below.

Turbulence shook Nathanial in his seat. The plane lurched, violently thrusting his shoulders against his harness. The superfortress bucked like a manic bull determined to throw every last cowboy.

Over the roar of the engines and the pounding of the rain, thunder reverberated in his chest. He stared out the window, trying to get a good look at the cloud formations. A flash of bright light seared his eyes.

The weather officer let out a startled curse. "Whiskey Tango!"

The radar screen flickered, then went dead.

# Eighteen

They should have been back by now. Maddie paced the floor, and Sue Ellen sat by the phone reading, seemingly calm as could be.

Maddie never should have let Nate go out into that storm without telling him how she felt. She shouldn't have avoided his calls.

What if he never came back?

She made another lap around the living room. She kept telling herself not to worry. Pops was alive and well in the future. Pops would be fine, so Nate would be fine. Right? But this…this churning in her stomach, the trembling in her hands. *This* was why she couldn't marry a military man.

And also why she knew she'd be miserable without him.

"You're about to wear a hole in the floor." Sue Ellen looked up from her magazine. "I'm sure every-thing is fine. They'll call when they can."

Nana sounded calm, but Maddie knew better. Not

only from growing up with the woman but also from spending the past week with the younger version. Sue Ellen was just as worried as Maddie, though she tried hard to mask her anxiety.

Maddie tried praying again, but her thoughts and words kept tangling into an incoherent mess. She had to do something. Standing around waiting would get her nowhere. "Come on. We need to go down to the base."

Sue Ellen scoffed. "You think they're going to let us onto the flight line just because our beaus are a little late?" She shook her head. "It doesn't work that way."

The Air Force and all their rules. She tried a different angle. "But if we hang around, some fellow is bound to tell us something about what's going on."

"Maybe." Sue Ellen drew her lip through her teeth. "But what if they call and no one is here to answer? We'll miss them in passing."

She had a point. The inconvenience of not carrying a phone in your pocket. "Okay. You stay here, and I'll go. If I don't find out anything in an hour, I'll come back. If I do, I'll call you."

Worry filled her grandmother's eyes, but Sue Ellen nodded solemnly.

A quarter hour later, Maddie stood in front of a building by a gated area with a sign that warned no unauthorized personnel could pass. She bounced on her toes, trying to see past the buildings and onto the runway, but she had no idea what she was looking for.

She scanned the clear sky. No planes dotted the blue. Pops had said they would take a six-hour flight. They should have been back two hours ago.

Something was wrong.

Maddie spotted a young man scurrying toward her and hurried to intercept his path. "Sir! Excuse me!"

He glanced at her but didn't slow his trajectory toward the door.

"Please! I just want to know if the weather reconnaissance plane is safe. They're two hours late."

His steps slowed and his face dipped into a scowl. "And you are?"

"Mrs. Hall," she blurted before she could think better of it. "Captain Hall went up with the crew of the Magnolia Mayhem."

The man stopped. Her stomach clenched. He glanced back toward the flight line.

"Please," Maddie whispered.

"Last transmission says the aircraft was struck by lightning. All communications have been lost." He gave her a sympathetic dip of his chin. "Someone will call the families once we know more. I suggest you return home."

Before Maddie could say anything else, he disappeared inside.

Her heart thudded. This couldn't be happening. Had the plane gone down? Wouldn't they send a rescue team?

*Please, God.*

Maddie sprinted back through the base and to their apartment. She burst through the door, causing Sue Ellen to yelp.

"The plane was struck by lightning. They haven't heard from them," Maddie blurted out as she rushed inside.

Sue Ellen leapt to her feet and wrung her hands. "Oh no."

Panic filled Maddie's chest. She must have messed something up by coming here. She'd changed the course of history somehow. Pops wasn't supposed to be in a plane that went down during a hurricane.

Unless…

Unless *she* hadn't done anything at all.

Suspicion poked at her brain, probing and testing. Things she'd deliberately ignored demanded to be examined. The manual at the inn. Weird things Nate had said and the songs they both knew.

The night at the beach. Nate had asked her about the song. And music she'd played. Almost as though he knew she wasn't from his time.

She'd wondered, but dismissed the idea, figuring he asked so many questions because she had been so terrible at lying. So she'd avoided the subject to give herself time to think.

Truth be told, she'd avoided examining the suspicion because she'd been so sure Nathanial Hall was a man of class and sophistication from the post-war era.

Except, maybe he wasn't.

She groaned. Why hadn't she come right out and asked him?

If Nate wasn't from this time, then he shouldn't be on that flight. Why would he have gone up with them?

What if he was never supposed to fly into that storm and by joining he'd changed something?

"Maybe it only damaged their communications," Sue Ellen said, oblivious to Maddie's spiraling thoughts. "They could still be on their way home."

Maybe. "This wasn't supposed to happen." The back of her throat burned with tears she could not let loose. To let them consume her would mean defeat. And she still held out hope.

If only by a thread.

Sue Ellen placed a hand on Maddie's shoulder. "We never know what's going to happen, especially on missions like these." She turned Maddie to face her and searched her eyes. "You love him, don't you?"

The words stole Maddie's breath. She let out a nervous laugh. "How should I know? It's only been a week."

Sue Ellen lifted her eyebrows. "You can't get yourself worked up like this every time he goes out on a mission."

"That's just the point!" Maddie threw her hands into the air. "I don't want to always feel like this. Spend my life worrying. How can I survive that?"

"I suppose you'll have to leave the running of the world in God's hands." She offered a wry smile. "Besides, worrying doesn't give us any control."

Maddie stared at her. The words sounded simple. Yet difficult to follow. How did she *force* herself not to worry? How did she stop agonizing over making a wrong choice or fretting over the choices of others?

"I wish I'd been honest with him before he left. Instead, the last time we spoke…" She shook her head. "It didn't go well. I should have known better." She should have told him the truth, even if it did make her sound crazy.

Would he die in a storm, and she'd lose him forever? Maybe she could go back to The Depot. Start over. Come back but this time do things differently with Nate. Tell him how she felt about him without fear of losing him.

But that was ridiculous. She'd been back to that house twice and hadn't made it back to the future. What made her think she could go back and start this adventure again?

No. She was stuck here. Stuck waiting. Tears rolled down her cheeks.

Why was she so upset? Pops would be fine. He had to be or she wouldn't be alive.

But would Nate survive?

Sue Ellen rubbed her shoulder. "Why don't you

freshen up, and I'll make us some tea? We'll talk about what's really bothering you while we wait for them to call."

Numb, Maddie turned toward her room. She would tell Nana the truth. About where she came from and about all that had happened. Tell her everything. Decision made, she felt lighter.

Telling the truth, no matter how weird, would always be the best choice.

In the blue vintage bathroom, she splashed her face with water, trying to cool her heated cheeks. She reached for the hand towel and rubbed the cloth down her face.

The lights flickered.

She lowered the towel. The bathroom mirror shimmered.

What?

Her breath caught, and she took a step back. The silver metal rippled and expanded. Maddie sucked in a breath to scream.

Everything went black.

Dazed, Nathanial stared through the window as his mind ran through all of their problems. Communications down. Navigation equipment glitching. Weather radars possibly fried. And they'd be punching through to the eye any moment, too low.

"LT!" Nathanial shouted to the weather officer. "You got anything on radar?"

"No, sir." He shook himself, clearly rattled. "We are all down."

The lightning had to be the problem. With the communications out, they'd never radioed back, and if they flew into that eyewall too low, the risks could be detrimental. But how could he convince the crew that he knew their future?

"Got a good look at that cell when the lightning flashed. You need to tell the pilot to pull up. If he enters that eyewall low, we're going to get sucked in."

The young man's eyes widened. He hesitated.

"Did you see the look of those cumulonimbus clouds?" Nathanial pressed.

The young officer shook his head. His brows drew low. "I was watching the radar."

"If you'd seen what I did, you'd know we'll bottom out that low. We have to turn around. If we continue to fly with these damaged systems, we won't be crossing the winds at the right altitude." He thumbed toward the window. "You know I'm right. Without proper readings, they're flying blind."

While planes were built to handle lightning strikes, something had happened with this one that screwed with the electrical systems. One second the radar would be up, the next the screen was frozen. They couldn't fly with unreliable data. Likely what had gotten them killed.

Lieutenant Preston paled and switched on his com. "Adjust altitude! We're hitting this eyewall too low. Winds are unstable and storm clouds indicate severe turbulence."

The plane shuddered. One agonizingly long heartbeat later, the big girl shifted and rose. Nathanial could only pray it would be enough.

"Major MacBride," the LT said, "all weather recon systems are malfunctioning. If we continue this mission, we'll be sending in faulty information." The weather officer cut one last glance at Nate and dipped his chin in acknowledgment. "I suggest we set course to return to base immediately. The next crew will have to collect accurate readings."

Winds screamed over the wings, shuddering what now felt like their metal coffin. Nathanial prayed they could pull up in time. That they'd get above the worst of the turbulence and then be able to get this convulsing metal bird back through the storms to Keesler.

"Approximately five miles from center," the navigation officer said, his voice tight with concern. "Major, your orders?"

The plane lurched. Could Mac get this big plane pulled up before—

Nathanial's stomach clenched as the undeniable feeling of weightlessness sucked his breath away.

They were dropping out of the sky.

He braced himself. He'd failed. They were still going down, and there hadn't been a thing he could do about it. All he'd done was sign himself up for a flight into eternity.

*God, please look after my family. After Maddie and—*

The floating sensation abruptly ended as the plane bucked.

"All long-range communications are down, sir." The copilot said. "We've lost contact with base."

"Hold on!" Mac shouted. "We'll have to punch through and turn her around in the eye. Plot us a trajectory out of here."

The nose of the plane heaved upward, tilting the giant toward the atmosphere. Nathanial's throat constricted. A brief flash of lightning broke through the darkness, illuminating the tight features on the weather officer's face. The thunder boomed so close it swelled over the deafening noise of the plane and vibrated through his chest.

After what seemed like an eternity but couldn't have been more than three minutes, the dark gray clouds outside the window brightened.

A blinding white light poured through the window. The storm evaporated, the hiss of heavy rain shut off as if God had turned a faucet.

They slowed as they entered the eerie calm in the center of a convulsing circle of angry dark clouds. Miles above, the sky opened into a pristine blue.

"We've entered the eye," Lieutenant Preston announced. He gave Nathanial a relieved grin.

Relief surged through him. They'd made it into the eye alive. They'd pulled up in time.

Now, all they had to do was punch back through into a wall of heaving thunderstorms and make it back to base.

Without weather radar and communications.

# Nineteen

Maddie awoke with a start. Her head pounded, and she groaned. "What in the world?"

She rolled to her side as her alarm played a cheery tune, the music trying to punch through the fog in her brain. Why did her head hurt? Where was she anyway? Slowly, recognition sprouted and took root.

Her alarm.

On her cell phone.

She lurched upright. No. No, no, no!

Maddie grabbed the phone and slid her thumb to shut it up. Six a.m. October sixteenth. The day of the party. She stared at her phone. Her throat scorched and she tried to swallow, but her mouth had become the Sahara. She was back in her room at the B&B. On the morning of her grandparent's sixty-fifth wedding anniversary.

What about the storm? The flight? What had happened to the crew?

Had it all been a dream?

As the pain in her head receded, Maddie fumbled around the room. No way had the past week been a dream. No one remembered dreams that vividly. Nobody felt the ache deep in her heart over a man who wasn't real.

Did they?

Maddie threw on her clothes and grabbed her broken suitcase. She lumbered along the hall, lurched down the stairs, and hurried to the kitchen.

Mrs. Easley sat sipping a cup of coffee in the homey kitchen. She looked up, her eyes sparkling. "Have a good night, dear?"

Maddie stared at her. "I, uh, had a really weird dream." Awkward. How did one start a conversation asking a woman if she knew her house transported people through time?

Mrs. Easley nodded as if that hadn't been a strange thing to say. "Ready to check out?"

"Yes, ma'am." She shifted her feet. "You, um, well, no one else here had any crazy dreams, did they?"

The woman took another sip of her coffee. "Dreams? No, I don't believe anyone has mentioned any dreams."

A sinking feeling settled in her stomach. Had the last week really been nothing but one long, ridiculously vivid dream?

Only one way to find out.

She checked out of The Depot and hurried to her

car. Nana would know. Nana would remember.

At six thirty-five, she was knocking on Nana's door. She scanned the street. Normal, modern cars. The beachy bungalow looked the same. Nana's hanging pots filled with flowering vines couldn't belong to an identical older woman.

Had anything changed? Would she find different people living in this house? Would Nana be married to someone else? Questions stung her like a hive of swatted bees, each prick stinging. Her stomach churned, and each breath seemed harder to draw than the last.

Seconds ticked by like hours. Her heart hammered. They would be gone. Nana married to that other man from the dance. Her mother wouldn't have been born.

She would float in some out-of-time limbo with no family and—

No. She forced herself to calm down. Worrying wouldn't bring her control. She breathed deeply. Prayed God would walk with her through whatever the next moments, days, and years would bring.

When she thought her ribs would crack under the beating of her heart, the door finally opened.

Nana's familiar face smiled at her. "My. Aren't you early."

Maddie launched herself into Nana's arms. She was here! The woman Maddie had loved her entire life still lived in this house, on this street. In this time. A sense of home enveloped her. No matter what else happened, at least she hadn't lost Nana.

Nana caught her and pulled her close. "What happened? Are you all right?"

Maddie pulled back, afraid to ask but desperate to know. "Where's Pops?"

"In the kitchen." Nana frowned. "What's going on?"

Ignoring the question, Maddie hurried inside, barely taking in the coastal furnishings that hadn't changed. She bolted into the kitchen to find Pops tapping a spoon in his coffee.

Robert MacBride. *Her* grandfather. Her knees wobbled, and she had to grab one of the barstools to keep her balance. He hadn't disappeared.

Nothing had changed.

Her insides twisted again. Having lost them would have been devastating. But then, not having found Nate ripped the melody from her heart. The pang curdled in her throat and brought the sting of tears to her eyes. So did that really mean she'd dreamed everything?

Pops's smile faded. "Hey there, kiddo. You all right?"

He was here. Alive. Fine. Survived the storm—or maybe never flew into a hurricane at all.

"Uh, Pops. Can I ask you something?" She tucked a strand of hair behind her ear and glanced at Nana as she shuffled past, still in her bathrobe.

"What's bothering you, pumpkin?" He set his mug

down and studied her.

"Did you ever fly with the Hurricane Hunters?"

Nana and Pops shared a glance. "I did. Fifty-three to fifty-six. Why?"

Had that always been in the past? "How come you never told me?"

Pops shrugged. "Transferred out and started flying other reconnaissance work. Why do you ask?"

This was going to sound crazy. "Did you fly with a man named Captain Nathanial Hall into Hurricane Flossy?"

Pops drew his head back as though the question had reached out and bitten him. His eyebrows drew together, creating additional wrinkles across his forehead.

"Where did you hear that name?" Nana asked, rounding the table and coming to stand by Pops.

Maddie ignored her. "Did you?"

"He flew one mission with us." Pops drew out the words, running a hand down the scruff on his chin.

"And?"

"Lightning hit our plane. Messed with the instruments. Weather officer said if not for Hall's experience, we would have entered the eyewall too low and probably wouldn't have made it into the eye alive."

Mouth dry, Maddie could only stare at him.

"Turns out it was a good thing we swung her around and aborted early. Got three miles from shore before system malfunctions sent us down into the ocean." He scratched the back of his head. "If we'd kept flying our passes through the center, we probably would have crashed in the middle of the hurricane. Doubt we would have survived. God was looking out for us that day by letting Captain Hall onto the manifest."

The way he spoke—with a reverent sadness—had Maddie's eyes burning. "What happened then?"

Pops shook his head. "Rescue teams searched for three days. We never found Captain Hall."

Nana gripped his arm, her eyes sad.

"If not for him, I don't know if any of us would have survived. His quick thinking and sharp eye likely saved five lives."

"Your grandfather never flew with the Hurricane Hunters again." Nana watched Maddie with keen eyes. "Where did you hear about Captain Hall?"

Maddie sank onto a chair, blood thrumming in her ears.

Gone.

Nate was gone. And not just separated from her by time or age. Tears slipped down her cheeks. She swiped them away. At least she knew now. The time in the past hadn't been a dream. She wouldn't have dreamed Nate. Wouldn't have known about the flight into the storm.

But why? Why send her there only to force her to feel this pain?

Nana placed a hand on her shoulder, and Maddie

searched her face. The same face of her friend, just with a few wrinkles. "Do you remember," she whispered.

"Remember what?"

"Your roommate from that time."

Nana stared at her, a strange light sparking in her eyes. "Maddie." She pressed her lips tight as though trying to keep something in. Finally, she let out a breath. "I always loved the name. Suggested it to your mother." She shared another look with Pops. "Then as you got older…well, it always seemed funny how much you looked like her."

Or had *been* her.

"What happened to her?" The words barely squeezed through her throat.

"I don't know," Nana said. "She disappeared the same day Captain Hall died."

Nathanial awoke with a start. What in the world? He lurched up from his bed at The Depot.

Six-thirty.

He grabbed his phone. Sixteen October. The day of his exam. His head throbbed. What had happened? The last thing he remembered was that the Magnolia Mayhem had made it out of Flossy alive. They'd been heading back to base.

There'd been a sudden drop. And then…nothing. He'd woken up here. He pushed the haze from his mind. Tried to force himself to focus. Scattered questions and disjointed thoughts crowded his skull, each one vying for attention but flitting quickly away.

He'd been in the middle of a hurricane but woken up in his bed. The sheets were soaked in sweat. His pulse galloped.

A dream?

Couldn't have been. No dream was that real. Never in his life had he lived an entire week in a dream. Remembered the moments with such detail. He'd been there. Traveled through time.

Maddie.

The thought of her brought an ache. What had happened to her? Was she still there in the past, waiting for him to return from the mission? Had the rest of the crew survived? Made it to base? What would they think of him disappearing from inside the plane?

Had he saved them?

He threw on his uniform and bolted out the door, ignoring the throbbing pain in his head. Downstairs, he found Mrs. Easley in the kitchen, sipping coffee.

"What happened?" He barked.

Mrs. Easley lifted graying eyebrows, looking exactly as she had the weeks he'd stayed here during training. "What do you mean?"

"In 1956."

She sipped her coffee and regarded him over the rim. "Hmm. Let's see. I remember a hurricane from that year. I believe I took that week to go visit some friends." She nodded toward a clock on the wall. "Don't you have an exam this morning?"

"Was she here?"

"Was who here?"

"You know, don't you?" There was something about the way she talked. The calm manner in which she spoke. She had been there. Driven him to the base. Or at least, the younger version of her had. He didn't know how all the pieces of this puzzle fit, but this woman might. "How does it work?"

Mrs. Easley set her mug on the counter. "There are a lot of things in this world we don't control, Captain Hall. Things beyond our understanding and outside of our influence."

Figured. A cryptic answer. "How did you do it?" He leaned on the counter. "How can I go back?"

"That's above my pay grade, Captain." Her smile seemed apologetic. He was about to protest, but she held up a hand. "I merely run The Depot. Man the station, as it were. I'm not the Conductor."

The words sent a chill down his spine, and he leaned away. His chest burned, and the question slipped out as nearly a whisper. "Will I see her again?"

Mrs. Easley's warm eyes held compassion. "That's not up to me, son."

"Was she here? Did she travel to the past as well?"

Another sad smile and no answer.

Pain wrenched in his heart. He'd chosen to go on the mission without declaring his feelings and now he'd probably never see her again. He rubbed his chest as though that could ease the pain.

He'd lost her, and he didn't even know if the mission had succeeded. What if he'd lost her and they'd still died? Had he failed in everything?

He turned away and headed back toward the stairs. Would his textbook still show the Magnolia Mayhem going down in Flossy?

"What about your exam?" Mrs. Easley called after him.

He'd be late if he didn't go now. But he had to know. He dashed up the stairs. He'd grab his manual. Would the information have changed? Would the section somehow now say the plane had returned safely? Minus one soul onboard who had mysteriously disappeared?

He thrust open the door he hadn't bothered to lock and strode for the desk. His book lay closed.

With a note on top.

# Twenty

The story poured out of Maddie like water over Niagara Falls. The more she told, the stiffer Pops became and the paler Nana looked. They'd exchanged glances at several points, but once she'd started, she couldn't stop.

Finally, she sucked in a breath. "I was going to tell you," she said to Nana. "That day when you sent me to freshen up while you made tea. I…never got the chance."

They sat around the kitchen table, the air heavy with the weight of emotions Maddie had unloaded. She waited. How would they take her story? If anyone in the world were to believe she'd really lived in the past, these two would.

Nana fiddled with the edge of her robe. "After my roommate"—she kept her gaze on Pops—"went to freshen up, the phone rang." She lifted a shaky hand and brushed hair behind her ear. "It was you. I yelled to Maddie that you were headed to medical and told her to meet me at the base. She never came. When I got back to the apartment, all of her things were gone." Nana's voice had a faraway sound. "I always thought she'd heard about Captain Hall and couldn't take the news. I tried to find her, but I never saw her again."

Pops was staring at Maddie. "I never thought about it, but she does look an awful lot like that girl." He shook his head. "But what you're saying is impossible."

Nana's voice was gentle, almost placating. "How did you find out about all of that?"

"I was there." Maddie forced a laugh. "I wanted to see how you two ended up together." She shook her head. "It wasn't quite as fanciful as you always made it seem."

Pops chuckled gently. "After nearly dying in that storm, I realized life was short. I realized I might not have all the answers and the timing might not be perfect, but I wanted to take a chance with your grandmother. Proposed after a few dates and had to convince her I'd be worth the risk."

Nana's eyes shone. "You still are."

Tears burned at the back of Maddie's throat and slid down her cheeks. Her chance at a love like that had probably died in that storm. Nate was gone.

*Is he?*

Hope bubbled as a sense of gentle peace drifted over her. Maybe not.

Conversations they'd had, how'd they'd danced

around the subjects of music and pop culture, peppered her mind. Had she actually lost him? Or had he slipped through time as she had? "I keep wondering, though, if the same thing happened to him. If he—"

A knock sounded at the door.

Pops rose. "I'll get it. Probably Sadie trying to set up for that party twelve hours early," he grumbled.

Nana reached across the table and grabbed Maddie's hand. "You love him, don't you?"

Those had been the same words Nana had asked a few hours—no, sixty-five years—ago. Did she? "I think so."

Nana's eyes filled with tears. "Do you think maybe he—" She stopped and tilted her head.

Laughter filled the house. Masculine laughter. Maddie and Nana shared a look, then both lurched out of their seats. Maddie hurried through the living room.

Pops stood at the front door, talking with someone on the bungalow's porch. "Come in."

He stepped back, and Maddie's breath left her lungs. "Nate!"

Maddie. She was here. Alive. And just as beautiful as the last time he'd seen her. She launched herself into his arms, and he pulled her close, breathing in the scent of her.

"What happened?" she asked. "I never thought I'd see you again. What about the plane? Where did you go?" Before he could utter a word, she pulled back, her eyes searching. "Why didn't you tell me?"

Words. He couldn't speak a single one. But words didn't matter. All that mattered was her in his arms. The nearness of her. He tilted her back and let himself drown in the sweetness of her. She froze, then sank into his kiss.

The world melted around them. Every hesitation, every fear. More things that didn't matter. Not when he had her in his arms. Whatever had happened to them, how ever they'd ended up in the past, they'd found each other.

And he would never let her go again. Because he loved her.

Her fingers tangled in his hair, and his heart swelled. He couldn't risk missing a single moment. Who knew how many they had? One thing he'd learned through this adventure—he had no control over what tomorrow would bring. He could love Maddie in this moment and every moment after. He pulled back, brushing his lips against hers. "Marry me."

She gasped. "What?"

"I don't ever want to lose you again." He kissed her gently, then set her right. Her luminous eyes stared at him. Older versions of the friends they'd made in the fifties stood off to the side, silently watching. Her grandparents. All of her interest in them made perfect sense now. He laughed to himself. To think he'd wondered if she'd been in love with Mac.

Maddie stood before him, still staring, eyes uncertain. Something told him that he had to fight for her, had to lay his heart bare and hold nothing back. He couldn't promise her that life would be easy or things would always work out, but he could promise her all of him.

"Maddie." He took her hands in his. "I've known you one week and six decades. And maybe this is too sudden. But I don't want to take any moment for granted. Time can change so quickly. I don't know what will happen to us or how our lives will turn out. All I know is I want to love you every moment God grants me."

Behind her, Mac wrapped an arm around Sue Ellen and pulled her to his side. They had made it. God willing, he and Maddie would as well.

Tears rolled down her perfect cheeks.

"Marry me, Maddie." He dropped to one knee. Totally unprepared. Completely terrified. But he couldn't let her go. Not another second could pass without declaring everything she'd done to his heart. "Marry me and I will love you for every breath God gives me. Marry me and I promise to fight for you, for us, every day of my life. I promise to love you through every difficult day life throws at us. Through good times, hard times, and strange trips to the past. Wherever God sends us in this life, I want the honor of having you by my side."

She hadn't moved. Hardly looked as though she was breathing. His chest tightened. He'd offered her everything he could. He could only hope she felt the same, that she could see herself with him and—

Her sudden laugh cut off his thoughts. With tears streaming down her face, Maddie said, "Yes. I'll marry you, Nate."

His pulse roared through his veins. He swept her into his arms and kissed her again. A kiss to seal the promise of a lifetime together.

# Epilogue

*One year later*

Maddie hummed to herself as she pinned one side of her hair in a sleek fifties style. Leaning close to the mirror, she swiped on vibrant red lipstick and then inspected her reflection.

Perfect.

She'd had the dress made specifically for tonight. The shimmering black fabric slung low across her shoulders, and the hem grazed her calves. Almost an exact replica of the dress she'd worn the night she and Nate had met.

Music swelled outside the door, and she could hear people's laughter. Seemed most of the guests had arrived. A twinge of nerves sent her skin prickling. They'd be performing tonight for a small crowd of friends and neighbors. A joint-delayed reception to celebrate her and Nate's elopement and Nana and Pops's sixty-sixth anniversary.

She couldn't think of a better way to celebrate her

young marriage than by honoring the marriage her grandparents had forged as an example.

Maddie stepped out of the bathroom at her grand-parents' bungalow and into a beautiful fall day on the manicured backyard. Decorations hung from the trees, and tables lined one side of the fence, layered with snacks and treats she and Nana had spent yesterday preparing. She greeted well-wishers as she made her way to her friend's side.

Abigail looked beautiful in a pale green dress, her long dark hair pulled into a thick ponytail. "There you are!" Abigail's blue-green eyes sparkled. "Don't you look charming? Like you stepped right out of the fifties."

Maddie laughed. "Thought it would be fitting, since my grandparents met in 1956." And recreating that night would be perfect for the party. For all four of them.

Her eyes snagged on Nate across the yard, and he offered a smile that turned her heart to mush. She wiggled her fingers at him.

Abigail followed Maddie's gaze. "Married life treating you well?"

"Best six months of my life," Maddie said with a laugh.

"Still mad I didn't get to be a bridesmaid," Abigail grumbled. "You were in too much of a hurry to get hitched."

Maddie laughed. "When you know, you know. Why wait?"

She sighed, looking a bit wistful. "I guess." She flipped her hair over her shoulder. "Anyway, good thing he got stationed here. Your grandparents would have hated for you to move away." She made a face. "Though I don't know how you deal with him flying into all those storms."

"I just take it one flight at a time and leave the rest in God's hands."

An Elvis tune played over the Bluetooth speakers, and her gaze darted back to Nate. He rolled his eyes at the same instant Maddie did. She laughed, loving how they could share moments like those. He waved at Pops to cut the music off so they could start their performance.

Abigail sighed. "How do I find a guy like that?"

Time travel to the past. "No internet dating." Maddie nudged her shoulder.

Now it was Abigail's turn to roll her eyes. "It's like you got lucky one day and *poof*. Mr. Right."

She opened her mouth to reply, but the sounds of Nate's guitar meant she'd better get on stage. She squeezed her friend's arm. "We'll talk after." A strange thought struck her. "And maybe I know somewhere you can visit. Might be exactly where you can find your own miracle."

Confusion scrunched Abigail's face, but Maddie

hurried off. It was time she told her friend about The Depot. The weird B&B had worked for her and Nate. Maybe Mrs. Easley had a room with Abigail's name on it, too.

Maddie took her place on the stage and enjoyed the appreciative way her husband's eyes lit. She sat at the piano, and her fingers caressed the keys. Nate strummed along to the jaunty tune about lasting love, and then his rich voice carried on the air. Better even than Ol' Blue Eyes himself. At least in Maddie's opinion.

Maddie's heart swelled when Pops led Nana to the center of the grass. They grinned at one another as they swayed.

Pops gave Maddie a wink and nodded to Nate. She grinned in return. Just as Nana and Pops's love had been meant for "ever and a day," so would be hers and Nate's.

One moment at a time.

# Books by Stephenia H. McGee

## Ironwood Plantation
*The Whistle Walk*
*Heir of Hope*
*Missing Mercy*
*\*Ironwood Series Set*
\*Get the entire series at a discounted price

## The Accidental Spy Series
\*Previously published as The Liberator Series
*An Accidental Spy*
*A Dangerous Performance*
*A Daring Pursuit*
*\*Accidental Spy Series Set*
\*Get the entire series at a discounted price

## Stand Alone Historical Titles
*In His Eyes*
*Eternity Between Us*

## Contemporary
*The Cedar Key*

# Time Travel

*Her Place in Time*
(Stand alone, but ties to Rosswood from The Accidental Spy Series)

*The Hope of Christmas Past*
(Stand alone, but ties to Belmont from In His Eyes)

# Novellas

*The Heart of Home*
*The Hope of Christmas Past*

www.StepheniaMcGee.com
Sign up for my newsletter to be the first to see new
cover reveals and be notified of release dates
New newsletter subscribers receive a free book!
Get yours here
bookhip.com/QCZVKZ

# About the Author

Award winning author of Christian historical novels, Stephenia H. McGee writes stories of faith, hope, and healing set in the Deep South. She's a homeschool mom of two boys, writer, dreamer, and husband spoiler. Stephenia lives in Mississippi with her sons, handsome hubby, and their fur babies.

Visit her website at www.StepheniaMcGee.com and be sure to sign up for the newsletter to get sneak peeks, behind the scenes fun, the occasional recipe, and special giveaways.

Facebook: Stephenia H. McGee,
Christian Fiction Author
Twitter: @StepheniaHMcGee
Instagram: stepheniahmcgee
Pinterest: Stephenia H. McGee

Printed in Great Britain
by Amazon